MURDER

The two men were locked frozen on the ground, Slocum on top of Corporal.

With a mighty and abrupt move, Slocum reversed their positions, throwing himself to the ground and pulling his opponent over with him, even as the shot that Slocum had expected Burns to pull off split the night.

On top of him, Corporal went suddenly stiff.

"Goddamn it, Burns . . ." he said.

In the night, Rafer Burns laughed.

"Burns!" Slocum shouted, "You shot your own man!"

* * *

This book also contains a special preview of
the next exciting SLOCUM novel
by Jake Logan—
BOOMTOWN SHOWDOWN

DON'T MISS THESE
ALL-ACTION WESTERN SERIES
FROM THE BERKLEY PUBLISHING GROUP

THE GUNSMITH by J. R. Roberts

Clint Adams was a legend among lawmen, outlaws, and ladies. They called him . . . the Gunsmith.

LONGARM by Tabor Evans

The popular long-running series about U.S. Deputy Marshal Long—his life, his loves, his fight for justice.

LONE STAR by Wesley Ellis

The blazing adventures of Jessica Starbuck and the martial arts master, Ki. Over eight million copies in print.

SLOCUM by Jake Logan

Today's longest-running action Western. John Slocum rides a deadly trail of hot blood and cold steel.

JAKE LOGAN

SLOCUM AND THE LADY 'NINERS

BERKLEY BOOKS, NEW YORK

SLOCUM AND THE LADY 'NINERS

A Berkley Book / published by arrangement with
the author

PRINTING HISTORY
Berkley edition / April 1995

All rights reserved.
Copyright © 1995 by The Berkley Publishing Group.
Material excerpted from BOOMTOWN SHOWDOWN by Jake Logan
copyright © 1995 by The Berkley Publishing Group.
This book may not be reproduced in whole or in part,
by mimeograph or any other means, without permission.
For information address: The Berkley Publishing Group,
200 Madison Avenue, New York, New York 10016.

ISBN: 0-425-14684-7

BERKLEY®
Berkley Books are published by The Berkley Publishing Group,
200 Madison Avenue, New York, New York 10016.
BERKLEY and the "B" design
are trademarks belonging to Berkley Publishing Corporation.

PRINTED IN THE UNITED STATES OF AMERICA

10 9 8 7 6 5 4 3 2 1

SLOCUM AND THE
LADY 'NINERS

1

Another ride out.

In his saddle, on his tired Appaloosa, Slocum sighed.

How many rides out had he made the last few weeks?

The last few months?

Can't even remember.

It was true: There'd been so many comings and goings lately, so many dusty towns entered and left behind, with nothing in between to remember them by, that now Slocum couldn't remember where he'd just been and where he was supposed to be going.

You're tired, John, he told himself.

Maybe you're just plain used up.

1

Not even having the energy to argue with himself, Slocum merely nodded, and sighed again.

Seeming to read his mind, his Appaloosa snorted, kicking his tired gait through the dust as he tramped on.

Now Slocum yawned, even though sundown was still hours away, and suddenly he wanted to climb down from his mount and take a snooze right there.

"Hold up, boy," he said to his horse, and once again the mount seemed to read his mind, because he had already stopped dead, waiting for Slocum to crawl down off his back.

Yawning again, Slocum slid down from the saddle, tiredly pulled his bedroll after him, and laid it out right in the shadow of his horse.

"Don't go away," Slocum said, barely able to keep his eyes open, knowing that he was breaking most of his own rules in not attending to his mount, not checking and cleaning his weapons, not doing all of the other little things that had kept him sharp and alive all these years.

Take care of it later, he thought.

Yawning once more, Slocum nodded to his own thoughts and lay down, rolling himself up to sleep.

Head on his side, he stared back over the dusty road, toward the town he had just left, not two hundred yards behind him.

What was it called?

Yawning, he couldn't remember.

Peterson?

Paducah?

Who cares?

Nodding as he closed his eyes, he smiled slightly as he gave himself over to dreams of riverboats, desperate fights with desperadoes, the kisses of beautiful women, and a hundred other adventures he had participated in, in what seemed like another life, lived by another man, not the John Slocum who had lived the last few months in increasing boredom, riding from town to town in aimlessness.

Fleetingly, the vision of the town he had just left, the dusty, tired shops fronting a tired street trudged by tired people, flashed through his mind.

What was it called?

What state was it in?

Arkansas?

Texas?

Was he even in the United States?

Don't know.

Don't care.

Slocum snored, in the late day, in a place whose name or location he couldn't remember, and for a while his dreams returned to those other exciting places he had been, in those other exciting times, before the crack of what sounded like a rifle shot—maybe the one

that would finally put an end to John Slocum—
woke him from his reverie and put all boredom
and tiredness firmly behind him.

Instantly on hearing what sounded like the
crack of a rifle shot, Slocum was on his feet. He
was like a machine, throwing the bedroll aside
even as he reached for the Winchester rifle in
its scabbard, mounted behind the saddle on his
Appaloosa.

Eyes sharp and ready, trigger finger becoming
part of the rifle itself, Slocum was ready to fire
and protect himself, even as the sleepy dreams
he had been immersed in—something involv-
ing a redheaded girl in El Paso, and gold—faded
into the now-fading day.

Slocum heard laughter and shouting as he
returned to this world—and then there was
another crack and something white and much
larger than a bullet came flying over his head.

Still ready, Slocum looked up from behind his
Appaloosa to see a caravan of wagons stopped
not fifty yards from him, and a swarm of people
rushing out from the town toward it.

Relaxing a bit now, Slocum turned to look
at the round white thing, which had landed
twenty feet away and lay still on the ground.

"Hey, mister!" a voice called. "Throw the
ball back!"

Slocum turned to see someone gesturing to
him, a young gal waving a long, smooth stick.

Cautiously, Slocum approached the white object and picked it up.

"Throw it back, please!" the gal with the stick called.

Slocum examined the sphere, finding it vaguely familiar, leathery, and hard, then, transferring his Winchester to his left hand, he threw the object back at her.

It bounced in the dust in front of the girl, who snatched and caught it with her own free hand.

"Thanks, mister!" the girl called, then she turned away from Slocum, tossed the sphere in the air, and hit at it with the stick.

"Well, I'll be—" Slocum began, but then there was a hard tap at his shoulder, and he turned to see a bright-eyed, short, rotund man staring up at him.

"You on the team, mister?" the man asked excitedly.

As Slocum regarded him, the man looked at the Winchester in Slocum's hand and laughed.

"Guess not. That ain't no baseball bat. You got a pretty good arm, though!"

Still laughing, the man turned from Slocum and waddled excitedly toward the parked wagons.

Pushing his hat back and shaking his head in wonder, Slocum followed the little man to see what all the commotion was about.

• • •

Slocum thought he'd seen everything. He'd
seen bank robberies, riverboat card games with
millionaire's stakes on the table, the horrors
of war and the subtler horrors of peace, con
men of every sort, murderers and thieves of
every description—the whole human carnival
set out before him as if on a plate.

But John Slocum had never seen anything
quite like this.

At first he thought he'd stumbled into the
middle of a circus show. He'd seen circuses
before. But if this was a circus, where were
the tents and animals and sideshow stands?
Here there were only two wagons, and girls—
including the one who had waved the stick at
him—in funny-looking outfits.

And one more woman, sitting alone in the
front wagon, and just about the prettiest girl
Slocum had ever seen, in ribbons and bows,
with green eyes that flashed a little bright-
er when they briefly met Slocum's, before he
turned away to look again at the goings on.

The gals in outfits were marking off a flat,
wide spot in the desert, and throwing the white
sphere around, or catching it after the girl with
the stick hit it to them.

"Yep, that there's baseball!"

Slocum looked down to see that the excit-
able round little man had stopped next to him,
and stood goggle-eyed looking at the spectacle

before him, thumbs in his suspenders.

"You mean they're going to play here?" Slocum said.

The rotund man spit tobacco juice and then wiped his mouth with his sleeve.

"You bet! And there's gonna be lots of money to be made, too!"

Baseball! The game that Slocum had seen others play occasionally during battle lulls in the Civil War, which Slocum himself had played once or twice when there was nothing else to do, between the booming of the cannon and the flying of bullets—baseball!

"They play for gold?" Slocum asked, astounded.

The old-timer took his time answering, then spit tobacco again.

"Yep. Jus' about the biggest thing we ever seen here in Parker. A professional girls' baseball team. Travel the whole country puttin' on exhibitions and playing the best nine around. And they gonna play for money all right—*big* money." The old-timer pointed at the girl with the green eyes, who had turned them Slocum's way and now gave a little smile to go with them.

"And see that there girl, mister?"

"Yes," Slocum said, giving the green-eyed beauty a tip of his hat and a smile in return.

"She's just about the toughest thing on two long legs *you* ever seen."

"Is that so," Slocum said.

"Believe it, mister," the old-timer said. He spat tobacco juice again and ambled off. "And I wouldn't be surprised if there's big trouble 'fore all this is over. Big money and big trouble go hand in hand, mister."

Slocum glanced again at the girl in ribbons and bows, who once again met his eyes and smiled, as Slocum nodded, his boredom, along with the girl from El Paso who had haunted his dreams not ten minutes ago, already long forgotten.

"Is that so . . . ," Slocum said again, and smiled himself.

2

Slocum ambled over to the girl sitting in the wagon and tipped his hat.

"Evening, ma'am," he said.

She looked him straight in the eye, a wry smile on her face.

"Evening yourself, stranger."

"Name's John Slocum."

She nodded.

"Not a bad name," she said. Suddenly she reached out and grabbed his arm in a tight grip.

"Not a bad pitchin' arm, either."

"Ma'am?" Slocum said.

"Ever play baseball, Mr. Slocum?"

Slocum gave a short laugh.

"Little bit, during the War Between the States. A few boys'd get a game together, 'tween battles."

She let go of his arm, after holding it a little too long. Her grip had been as steady as the gaze from her green eyes.

"Played lately?"

Slocum laughed again. "Not likely," he said.

"You think it's silly, us being out here?" she said without humor.

"I didn't say that, ma'am . . ."

Her eyes flashed brief anger.

"Well, it's not at all," she said. "Everyone in the country will be playing this game before too long. There are leagues forming, professional ones, back east."

Her anger disappeared.

"Sorry, Mr. Slocum, I just get agitated at times."

"More like defensive, ma'am. Nothing wrong with that, if it's over something you believe in."

She looked at him with new interest.

"You seem okay, Mr. Slocum. Since you don't use a bat, you by any chance know how to use that gun of yours?"

She pointed at Slocum's Colt .45, nestled comfortably in its cross-draw holster.

"More than I wish sometimes, ma'am."

She waved a hand.

"Forget the 'ma'am' business. Name's Cotilda Murphy."

She put out her hand and shook Slocum's again, with a strong grip.

"You sure have got a strong set of fingers, Miss Murphy."

Her eyes lingered on Slocum's even as her grip, now softening, lingered.

"Interested in a job, Mr. Slocum?"

"Call me John."

"All right."

Slocum liked losing himself in her green eyes, and found himself nodding.

"Need a little protection, Miss Murphy?"

"It's Cotilda. And the answer is yes. We've been . . . bothered, now and then. And I've got good reason to believe we're going to be bothered while we're here."

Slocum saw that she still hadn't let go of his hand.

"I can offer you a little bit in the way of money, and of course all the grub you can wolf down and all the coffee you can drink."

"You have anything else to offer?" Slocum said, pushing his luck.

She suddenly noticed her limp hand in his and pulled it away, reddening for a moment in embarrassment.

And then suddenly her eyes were steady as steel again, and her wry smile was back.

"Could be, John."

She jumped down from the wagon, yelling

something to one of the ball players, who was throwing a ball too close to the swelling crowd, and now Slocum got a good look at her figure, which was lithe, petite, and at the same time looked to be as hard and strong as her grip and her gaze.

"Stick around, John," she said, as she walked toward the gathering ball players. "I'll make a batsman of you yet."

Cotilda Murphy pushed her way through the crowd, and Slocum followed. When she reached what were the beginnings of a ball field, she stopped at a round circle of dirt where the pitching mound would be and stopped.

She turned and faced the expectant townsfolk, the sinking sun behind her a soft backdrop for her small, strong frame.

"Listen up!" she said, and the townsfolk went silent. "You all know why we're here! For the next few days, we're going to bring a circus full of excitement to this part of Texas! Because this is a circus *you* get to perform in! Those of you who saw us back in Witier a couple years ago know how it works. We're the Fort Worth 'Niners, and we'll play the best nine you've got in these parts—for gold!"

A cheer went up at the prospect of gambling.

"Settle down!" Cotilda shouted, and the crowd noise subsided. "What we'll do is, for the next two days, we'll help you get your best team together. I want everyone to have a chance, and I want only your best out here when the big game is played! We'll start tryouts tomorrow, at nine o'clock sharp. Now, tomorrow's Friday, and I realize most of you have chores and work to attend to, but we'll be out here all day. And the next day's Saturday, and we'll be out here then, too! And then on Sunday, at noon sharp, we'll have the big game!"

Another round of cheers.

"Any questions?" Cotilda said.

A scrawny man, looking to be at least sixty, put his hand up.

"Yes, sir?" Cotilda said.

"What 'bout 'quipment?"

"You mean bats and balls and such?"

"And gloves?"

"Well, we've got a couple of fancy-made gloves, and we'll be happy to share them. Most of my team play with their bare hands. But all equipment will be shared equally. Fair enough?"

The scrawny man nodded. "Sounds fair," he said.

"What about judgin'?" a voice called out from the back.

"Judging, or umpiring, as we call it, will be by the most honest man we can find. You got a parson or such around here?"

A thin man stepped forward tentatively, wearing huge glasses and squinting.

"That would be me, ma'am," he said meekly.

Cotilda grinned.

"Well, Parson, you're our umpire."

"Oh, dear," he said.

A cheer went up.

"Let's hear it for Reverend Gates!"

"Hurrah!" the crowed said as one, and Reverend Gates, still embarrassed, stepped back into the crowd, smiling shyly.

"Don't worry, Reverend, it's an easy job," Cotilda said. "We'll teach you everything you need to know. Any other questions?"

"Yeah," said a gruff voice, belonging to a bare-chested, soot-covered fellow who looked to be the town blacksmith. He suddenly broke out in a smile. "Where do we spend our winnings!"

A huge roar went up, and someone shouted, "Let's go to Farley's Saloon and figure that out!"

There was laughter, and the crowd began to break up.

"Remember, nine o'clock sharp tomorrow!" Cotilda shouted.

Another roar went up, and now, as the sun's orb touched the desert horizon, the meeting broke up, scattering the townsfolk to their various habitations back in Parker and Cotilda's baseball players to their various tasks preparing for the night.

Cotilda and Slocum found themselves alone on the pitcher's mound, surrounded by the beginning of the playing field.

"And now, John," Cotilda said, taking Slocum's hand and leading him off into the coming night, "you and I have business to discuss."

3

Soon Cotilda and Slocum had left the baseball field behind, and stood away from the milling ball players, who were now gathered at one of the wagons, fixing a meal.

Cotilda looked up into Slocum's face, and smiled.

"You hungry?"

"Always," Slocum said.

Cotilda laughed, and suddenly she pressed herself close to Slocum, sliding her hand down behind his trousers as she did so.

"Maybe you can't tell," she breathed, "but I'm mighty hungry myself."

"So I see," Slocum said, as his member began to respond to her attention.

"My, my," Cotilda said, her breath coming faster, "you really *are* a batsman, John Slocum."

"Yes, ma'am," Slocum said, putting his own hands on her pert rump, which tightened as she pushed against him.

"These clothes seem to be an impediment," Cotilda said, and she suddenly pushed herself away from Slocum, climbing out of her duds in a flash. By the hint of growing moonlight, Slocum saw only the ribbons and bows which still adorned her hair.

"Now you, John," she said, nearly attacking Slocum to help him get out of his own clothes, only stopping to once again fondle his now-hard member and press it against her.

"Myself, I'm mighty hungry," Cotilda said, and now she took her fill of him with her mouth, kneeling on the ground and grabbing Slocum's buttocks as Slocum stood, feeling his balls begin to fill with tight need.

Sliding her mouth up over the tip of Slocum's cock, licking it deliciously, she pulled Slocum down on top of her and said, panting, "*Mighty* hungry, John."

Slocum felt her open beneath him, and before he knew it, her nether mouth was taking his hardness in, much as her other mouth had a moment ago.

Slick, hot, and wet, she began to buck beneath him.

"John!" she panted, her hard green eyes softening in need, her hands once more on Slocum's buttocks, straining to ram him even deeper into her recesses.

Rising to her need, Slocum became a machine, his rock-hard penis jamming long into her heated love area.

Her nether muscles tightened, then tightened even more around his shaft.

"I'm ready, John!" she huffed, distracted and wild. "I'm ready!"

"Whatever you . . . say, ma'am," Slocum grunted, pulling out to his cock's head before driving his long, wet, hardened pole so far into Cotilda that her mouth opened in a silent, ecstatic scream.

And now, at the end of the mighty thrust, as Cotilda mouthed a needful "Now!" Slocum let his love load fly, a gigantic white spurt of juice that drove up into the hottest recesses of her wet nest, forcing her to drive her nails into Slocum's buttocks and all but scream in ecstatic pleasure.

And as if to prove that Slocum had done his job for her, now, as Slocum's load continued to explode into her, Cotilda's middle began to burst with orgasm, rendering her nearly blind as her lithe, wet body bucked wildly beneath Slocum, giving him as wild a ride as any untamed filly.

"Oh, John! John!" she gasped, as their two

bodies rode out the thunderous waves together, Slocum's white cum driving into her own white spurts at their tight-locked middles.

"Oh!" Cotilda gasped, as they met the final crest together, hot juices mingling, before the delicious ride was ended, the tensions of love relaxed into dreamy release, and Cotilda lay back, spent and happy.

"Why, Mr. Slocum," she purred, "I do believe that was the finest ride I've ever had."

Slocum smiled.

Cuddling against him as Slocum continued to smile, Cotilda Murphy whispered, reaching gently for Slocum's already rehardening shaft, "And I do believe I'd like to ride again, if you don't mind."

In the dark, Slocum continued to smile.

"Why sure, ma'am—"

But at that moment a rifle shot—a real one, not the crack of a wooden bat against a baseball—split the night, and all thoughts of love were driven from Slocum's mind as he dove to pull his Colt .45 from the cross-draw holster that lay curled like a snake on the ground next to him.

"Did you see where the shot came from?" Slocum whispered fiercely to Cotilda Murphy, who was scrambling to climb into her clothes. Slocum himself pulled on his breeches and lay crouched and ready, searching the night with his sharp eyes.

"No, but I know who shot it—" Cotilda said, not finishing as another shot, off to the right and a good ways out in the desert, flared in the night.

"Whoever it is doesn't seem to want to get too close," Slocum said.

"It's just a warning," Cotilda said. "It's happened before."

Slocum noted the edge of fear in her voice.

"Somebody been stalking you?"

"Yes," Cotilda said. "His name's Rafer Burns, and he has a small band of thugs who travel with him. He—"

Another shot flashed in the night, this time far off to the left, followed by another somewhere in between.

"He seems to have his men with him now."

"If he does what he's done before, there'll be a few more shots, and then they'll leave for the night. But we'll see them again tomorrow."

"What's he looking for?"

Two more shots, followed closely by a third, split the still desert night. Slocum thought of firing back, but the fact that the shots didn't seem to be aimed at anyone in particular, and the fact that he didn't think it wise to let on that Cotilda had any firepower with her, made him hold off.

There was another shot, and then silence.

Slocum waited, but off in the distance he heard horses' hooves and muted laughter.

Then a loud, strong voice called out, "Hey, Cotilda! We're back, little lady! And I can't wait to see you!"

There was more laughter, and then the strong voice said, "See you soon!"

A final shot rang out, followed by far-off whoops and the clatter of retreating hooves.

In a moment the desert was completely silent again, except for the mumbling of the disturbed ball players, who had thrown themselves to the ground at the first shot and now slowly began to return to their pursuits.

Slocum began to pull the rest of his clothes on, meaning to ride out after them.

"Where are you going?" Cotilda said, putting her hand on his arm.

"I figure I'll see where they're camped out, find out if they mean any more harm tonight."

"There's no need," Cotilda said. "They'll be back tomorrow, just like they said."

"Well," Slocum said, pulling his shirt on, "I think I'd better check it out anyway—"

"Please don't," Cotilda said.

"Ma'am?" Slocum said, surprised by the fear that had abruptly entered this strong woman.

"It's hard for me to talk about," Cotilda said, and now Slocum saw in the faint night light that a tear was staining her pretty cheek.

Slocum waited.

"Are you sure it wouldn't be better if I faced

them now?" he asked. "Maybe I could scare them off."

"They'll just come back," Cotilda said, sounding doomed.

"I'll do whatever you want, ma'am," Slocum said.

In the night, he saw her smile faintly.

"You're a good man, John Slocum. There aren't enough good men in the world. Stay, and let me tell you the story of what these men have done to me and my girls, and what they'll try to continue to do."

Feeling her move trembling against him, Slocum knew that he now had no choice, and he sat beside her in the night, holding her in comfort, as she told her tale.

4

"I first heard of Rafer Burns," Cotilda Murphy said, as she lay her trembling body in John Slocum's strong arms, "after I formed my girls into a team in Fort Worth. This was two years ago. I've been smitten with baseball ever since my brother, Tom, brought back the knowledge of how to play from Lee's army in Virginia, where he was stationed during the war.

"Tom used to play all the time, to the point where he went off to St. Louis to try his hand in one of the professional leagues that started forming four or five years ago. I wanted to go with him, but he said that was silly, that girls couldn't play baseball. He said it was unladylike. And this was after I'd taught him nearly everything he knew about pitching a ball correctly."

She looked up at Slocum and smiled faintly. Already her trembling had decreased.

"But you know the way men are, John. They have an idea in their minds about the way the world should be, and nothing can change it. Girls didn't play baseball in my brother's world, and that was that.

"My mother, of course, agreed with Tom. My father was killed in the war, leaving us all but destitute, and sometimes I think that he would have been on my side. He was a bit like you, John Slocum, a good man with a good man's mind."

"Why, thanks," Slocum said, and now he felt her warm in his arms, her trembling all but gone.

But then Cotilda looked out into the dark night, and her trembling began to return with the memories.

"So Tom went to St. Louis, and then Rafer Burns appeared.

"He was a gentleman at first. He'd been around near the end of the war. Some said he was an outlaw, others said he was a drifter, but he was charming enough and the ladies seemed to abide him. And for some reason he took a particular fancy to me, though I never showed him any encouragement.

"And also he became enamored of baseball,

and began to play locally, which was where I saw him sometimes.

"Baseball had become something of a gentleman's game, but as with another gentleman's sport, horse racing, there seemed to be betting involved. Sometimes two teams would form, and wagers would be placed on the winner.

"This was where I got my idea for my team. Since as a lady I was not allowed to play, what if the entire team was made up of ladies? Would people come to watch such a spectacle? And I must confess the betting side of it was appealing to me also, since money was so hard to come by. Even now I send money back to my poor mother, who hates what I've done but is so needful.

"Even more sad and needful because of Rafer Burns . . ."

Now her trembling had completely returned, and for a few moments she couldn't speak.

"What did he do to you, Cotilda?" Slocum said softly.

"He murdered my brother! That was the first of his abominations. His attentions toward me had become stronger, to the point where I was forced to ask him to leave me alone. He refused, and only became more persistent. And then Tom returned to Fort Worth with his St. Louis team, and . . ."

"Go on," Slocum urged. "Telling it will ease the pain."

"The simple fact is that Rafer Burns killed my brother. Tom saw the inappropriate attentions that Rafer was paying to me, and took it on himself to tell Rafer to stop. The next morning, the day that Tom's professional team was to play a local team composed of Rafer Burns and some of his cronies, among others, my brother was found murdered in an alley. Rafer Burns was suspected, but there was no evidence, and he walked free."

"Then how do you know that he committed the murder?" Slocum asked.

"Because he *told* me he did, bragged to me about it, while he was . . ."

Slocum waited while she cried in his arms.

"What did he do to you, Cotilda?"

She looked up into Slocum's face, her cheeks covered with tears.

"He forced himself on me! And then he swore I would never be rid of him, that he would follow me forever! And that's what he's done, John—stalked me from town to town, playing the charmer, joining the town teams with his cronies, torturing me with his presence and his leer. His men have even gone after some of the girls, but there's never any evidence and the local law can never do anything about it."

She held Slocum close.

"He's an evil man, John!"

Slocum put his arms around her.

"He's that and more, Cotilda, and I promise that he'll never bother you again."

"Oh, if only I could believe that, John! But he's clever, and sly as a snake, and he's never let anyone catch him at the things he's done."

"His lucky streak is about to end," Slocum said, a hard edge coming into his voice.

"Oh, John," Cotilda said, "you're too good to be true . . ."

In a moment, exhausted, Cotilda Murphy was asleep against Slocum, who stared hard into the night, and knew that all boredom and inaction were gone, because he had another fight on his hands.

5

Slocum awoke from the deepest of sleeps to what sounded, once again, like a rifle shot.

Immediately he thought of Rafer Burns.

But instant return to the world told him that it was only the sound of a bat hitting a ball, and sure enough when he opened his eyes, ready to go to his Colt, lying beside him in its cross-draw holster, he saw one of the white spheres arcing overhead and heard the dismayed cry of the man who now had to chase the errant orb.

"Gosh darn it, Hartley!" an impatient voice shouted. "Di'n I tell you to keep the ball on the field!"

As Slocum sat up, Hartley, a tall, lanky man

in bib overalls, loped by with a crestfallen look on his face.

Stretching and yawning, Slocum got up and faced a world vastly different from the one he had gone to sleep in. Gone was the night, and with it was any hint of danger.

The baseball field, in fact, had nearly been completed; two of the Fort Worth 'Niners players were finishing up with a rake on what would be the pitcher's mound, and another gal was setting bases in place.

The field looked about as professional as you could get out on the edge of the Texas desert, with the sun already climbing and a hot day coming on.

Slocum spied Cotilda Murphy off at the farthest edge of the field, talking to a group of townsfolk. Already Parker, Texas, had shown up in force, and groups of men, boys, and even a few girls were scattered here and there, tossing balls in the air or trying to hit them with a bat.

The man who had so recently castigated poor Hartley for his performance was having his own hard time of it; Slocum recognized him as the general-store keeper in Parker, and the man, stout and squint-eyed, was having the devil of a time hitting a baseball with his stick.

When he finally did strike the ball, it once again flew over Hartley's head.

"For Pete's sake, Hartley!" the shopkeeper

shouted, as the lanky fellow once again ran by Slocum to retrieve the ball.

"Rotten boss . . . ," Hartley muttered, a look of disgust on his face which made Slocum chuckle.

He was about to make his way across the field to Cotilda Murphy when he looked back to see her nearly to him, a morning smile on her face.

"Feeling better?" Slocum said.

She nodded, continuing to smile. "Because of you," she said.

"Well, now—"

"I mean it, John. Thank you." She blushed slightly. "For everything."

Slocum touched his hat.

"Figure those desperadoes'll be along today?" he asked.

Cotilda's face clouded.

"They might. Or Burns might wait until tomorrow and move his boys into the town's team then. Another of his games is that he likes to beat my gals at the last minute, and take most of the pot."

"Bunch of ringers, eh?" Slocum said. "Like playing possum in a poker game, when you know you're the best around."

Cotilda nodded, and then suddenly put her hand on Slocum's arm, holding with her strong grip.

"I really do thank you," she said.

"I'll be here for you, Cotilda," he said. With a slight smile he added, "For whatever reason."

Her blush returned.

"Unfortunately, there's a lot of work to be done today. I have to at least give these townspeople an idea that they can beat my gals. I've got to warn you that the betting will get mighty heavy before all this is over, and there might be more work for you to do than merely keeping an eye on Burns and his gang."

Slocum said, "Whatever comes along, we'll handle it."

"Good."

She pointed toward one of the wagons, where a smoky griddle was still doing its work.

"Why don't you go on over and get yourself some breakfast? La Vonda is chef today, and she makes a mean flapjack."

"All right," Slocum said, and as Cotilda turned and walked away from him, he allowed himself to admire once again the lithe figure that went with her strong spirit.

Slocum knew right away the kind of gal he was running into as he approached La Vonda at the smoky griddle. She already had her eye on him and a wide smile on her horsey face.

She was a big girl with big bones, and Slocum knew she probably had that mischievous smile on her face most of the time.

"Well, hello, sweet thing," she said, giving Slocum the eye.

Slocum laughed.

"La Vonda?" he said. "I'm told you make a mean flapjack."

She preened with pride.

"Sure do. I can cook and sew, too, and I've been known to plow a field and fix a roof. You lookin' for the marrying kind of gal?" Again she gave him the eye.

Slocum laughed and shook his head.

"Just breakfast, if you don't mind."

La Vonda shrugged, already expertly pouring a line of griddle cakes, which spit and shot smoke into the morning air.

"I always ask," she said. She turned back to Slocum and winked. "Even though I notice that you and the boss hit it off pretty good already."

"Well . . ."

La Vonda smiled widely. "Don't you kid me! I know when she's happy, and she's happy now." A momentary cloud crossed her features. "Been a long time since that girl's been happy."

"Rafer Burns?" Slocum asked.

La Vonda looked quickly at Slocum. "She tell you about him?"

Slocum nodded.

La Vonda shook her head. "Boy, she must *really* like you, mister. She don't hardly talk to anybody about Rafer Burns."

"Well," Slocum said, leaning closer and confidentially toward the cook, "the fact is, you can call me John Slocum, and another fact is I'd like to take care of this Burns problem for your boss." He leaned even closer and whispered, "If you'll tell me how."

"Shoot!" La Vonda nearly shouted. "That's an *easy* one, Slocum!" She transferred her flapjack flipper to her left hand and made a shooting motion with her right. "Just get rid of Mr. Burns, and his men."

Momentarily she blushed.

"All except one feller name of Pokey Johnson, that is."

Slocum said, "He a special friend of yours?"

La Vonda's blush deepened.

"Let's just say he ain't like the others. He's a little . . . soft in the head, you might say. Sweet fellow, when he's not in with the rest of 'em. I think he could be redeemed. The rest of 'em are snakes, but Pokey's . . ."

Slocum waited.

"Well, he's *Pokey*. Kind of slow and amiable."

"He sweet on you, too?"

She turned away, feigning sudden interest in the griddle cakes to hide her even deeper blush.

"I'm just telling the truth, is all," she said.

She turned around with a tall stack of flapjacks on a plate, which she thrust into Slocum's hands.

"Here," she said. "And don't choke on 'em."

Slocum smiled at her.

"I'll remember what you said about Pokey Johnson," he said.

Instantly La Vonda brightened. "You're okay, John Slocum. Like I said, he ain't never harmed anybody, himself. He follows the rest of 'em like a dog, but he's never harmed a hair on anybody's head."

Slocum said, in all seriousness, "You think it would help at all if I rode out and had a little talk with this Rafer Burns fellow? You think he'd listen to reason?"

La Vonda guffawed. "Does a copperhead or rattler listen to reason? You poke a stick at that boy, and he's liable to add you to his list. He keeps a list in his head, is what he does. People he thinks have crossed him. And sooner or later they end up dead, and there's nobody to blame. He never leaves footprints—he's just like a snake that way, too. Never leaves a trail." She turned to clean at her griddle. "But they always end up dead."

"Thanks," Slocum said thoughtfully, and turned away.

"Slocum?" La Vonda called out to him.

He turned.

She said, "You remember your promise about Pokey, you hear?"

"I hear," Slocum said.

She grinned. "And you come see me hit

on Sunday, you hear? I'm the best hitter on the 'Niners. And I'll smack one just for you, okay?"

"Okay," Slocum said, laughing, and La Vonda laughed, too.

6

After breakfast, which he washed down with some strong, good coffee, Slocum attended to his Appaloosa, checked his weapons again, and saddled up.

To his surprise, there was Cotilda Murphy, giving him a hard eye.

"Where you fixing to go, John?" Slocum shrugged.

"Figured I take a little ride. Get the lay of the land, is all."

"You know you're lying to me. You're going out to check up on Rafer Burns—am I right?"

Grinning, Slocum looked down into her hard eyes.

"Can't fool you, can I?"

"Didn't I tell you about Rafer? Hell, didn't La Vonda tell you about him?"

Slocum's smile widened. "That woman'll talk about anything, anytime, anywhere. She told me a mouthful about a fella named Pokey Johnson."

Cotilda snorted, but said, "Pokey's okay, I guess. Only one of 'em, you be sure."

Serious now, Slocum said, "Don't worry about Rafer Burns, Cotilda. He's got you all spooked, and I figure it's time to end the spooking. Man like that doesn't like to be drawn out into the open, and I'd just like him to know that that's the way it's going to be around here. He's gonna act in the open if he acts at all."

Cotilda grabbed his hand. "He'll kill you, John."

"He can try. But if I change the rules on him, maybe it'll scare him off."

She looked haunted.

"Nothing will scare that animal off," she said.

Slocum gently took her hand away from his, and turned his horse around.

"Then it's time this little game of his ended," he said.

In a few moments, Slocum had left the town of Parker, and the little baseball diamond outside it, behind.

Once again he was in his element. He hadn't realized how much he'd really missed it: the hunt, the chase, the thrill of adventure. He knew now what had turned him into the sluggish, bored, slow-minded thing he had become: inaction. He was not made to sit in an easy chair and watch the grass grow—he needed action, and plenty of it, to keep the blood flowing in his veins. All these sleepy, dusty towns he had ridden through in the last few months had worked their poison on him because the whole country was becoming one vast, safe, inactive place. Like a blanket, the peace was settling over the continent, and Slocum knew that for a man like him that was deadly.

He wondered how much longer men like him would last in the United States of America. The territories were settling up; Indian trouble was all but a thing of the past; the gunfight seemed to be going the way of the caveman.

Slocum didn't feel old, but he felt as if the clock were turning, leaving him behind. Him and his kind of man, who craved— who needed—action. How much longer would it last?

Then he thought of Rafer Burns, and knew that perhaps it would never end after all. As long as there were men like Burns, there would be a need for men like Slocum.

And, Slocum knew, there would always be men like Rafer Burns.

Content in his philosophy, Slocum turned his mind to other things, like enjoying the desert and lighting up a prized Havana, pulling in the rich, deep smoke in a leisurely puff, and blowing it out again.

Hell, this was a good life after all.

It didn't take Slocum long to locate Rafer Burns and his band.

They were almost predictable, making their camp about two miles out from Parker, just far enough away to stay undetected, but close enough to make the ride in an easy one.

Slocum had seen this kind of thing again and again. After all, desperadoes might be bad men, but that didn't make them smart. There were certain patterns they all fitted, and one of them was to make the world as comfortable a place as possible for themselves—even if that meant murdering a bunch of people along the way.

Slocum counted four of them in camp, and one out on scouting duty.

He came across the scout first, asleep in the shade of his own horse, which was tied to a stunted cottonwood.

Slocum gave him wide berth, wondering if the snoring man with the hat on his face was Pokey Johnson.

But then he knew that no, that hadn't been Johnson, because Johnson was no doubt entertaining the other three in camp, since as Slocum drew near he saw three men torturing a fourth, holding him down while dangling a snake over his face.

Slocum was able to ride right up on them, keeping a resting hand on the Winchester, which he slipped, ready, out of its scabbard and lay across his lap.

"Snakes get pretty riled up when you bother 'em in the daytime," Slocum said amiably.

The three men jumped in surprise; the one holding the snake let it fly and it landed a good yard away, slithering off in anger.

"What in hell—" one of the men said, going for his gun.

Slocum swiveled the barrel of the Winchester around on his lap, pointing it in the man's general direction.

Another of the men said in a commanding voice, "It's all right, Corporal. We don't want any trouble here."

The speaker was well-dressed, polite-looking, with a nearly handsome face and trim mustache.

Only his eyes were hard and black, and Slocum knew at once that this was Rafer Burns.

Burns bowed at the waist. "Hope we didn't bother you with our sport, stranger."

He looked down, smiling at the man on the ground, who scrambled to his feet, mumbling and dusting himself off.

"We didn't hurt you then, did we, Pokey?"
Burns said agreeably.

Pokey looked at Burns with anger that quickly turned to fear, and then looked away, mumbling.

Burns turned his amiable look on Slocum.

"Just a little daytime sport," he said, "to break the boredom."

He stepped forward, holding out his hand. "My name is Rafer Burns. And you . . . ?"

Slocum declined to take the hand, but while keeping his Winchester pointed in Burns's general direction, he slipped his Colt out of its holster and pointed it behind him.

Slocum said in a friendly voice, "Mr. Burns, I'd tell that fella sneaking up behind me, the one who was taking a snooze under a cottonwood three minutes ago, to turn back and finish that snooze." Slocum smiled. "I'd hate to have to end his snoozing forever."

Still smiling, Burns waved a hand and said, "You heard the man, Curt! Go back to sleep!"

For a moment everything was held suspended, and then Slocum, not sensing movement, cocked the Colt.

Laughing, Burns said, "He means it, Curt!"

"Shucks," Curt said, and now Slocum heard him retreating.

Burns sighed happily. "I apologize, Mr. . . ."

"Slocum."

"Yes, of course, Mr. Slocum. And you've met

everyone here except for Mr. Fontaine, my other associate—"

Fontaine, a grizzled character, merely returned Slocum's stare.

With a florid gesture, Burns asked, "Would you care to spend some time with us, Mr. Slocum?" He turned to Pokey. "Perhaps you could rustle up something for us to dine on, Mr. Johnson?"

Pokey stopped his mumbling long enough to say, "Sure, Mr. Burns. Whatever you say."

"That's all right," Slocum said. "I won't be eating with you, and I won't be staying long. Just wanted to get a good look at you, is all."

For the first time, Slocum saw anger and surprise, quickly suppressed, arc across Burns's features.

Burns looked up at Slocum, smiling. "Oh? You know of myself and my merry band, Mr. Slocum?"

"Yep."

"Are you by any chance the law in nearby Parker? I didn't see a badge . . ."

"I'm not the law. But I'm laying a little down for you."

Burns feigned surprise this time. "I'm afraid I don't quite understand . . ."

Slocum re-aimed his Colt behind him and pulled off a quick shot.

"Hey," a startled voice said, "you almost hit me!"

Slocum said, "I told you I wanted that man to go back to sleep." Slocum looked into Burns's hard eyes. "Get him around here where I can see him, or he'll sleep forever."

In a serious tone, Burns said, "Come on over here, Curt."

"Tell him to throw his gun down in front of me," Slocum said.

"Toss the firearm, Curt," Burns said.

"Aw, Boss . . ."

"Do as I say," Burns said, distinctly pronouncing each word.

Slocum heard the gun cock behind him, and now he pulled off another shot, dead on aim.

Curt groaned, and then there was silence.

"I take it that was some sort of code?" Slocum said. "Like when you said, 'Do as I say,' it meant take a shot at me?"

Burns, his face livid with controlled rage, said, "You shot my man!"

Pokey ran by Slocum to investigate and called out, "He's dead, Mr. Burns!"

Burns said in cold rage, "I don't know who you are, Slocum, or what you want, but I can tell you I won't forget this."

"Add me to the list in your head," Slocum said evenly.

Now Burns's eyes nearly glowed with venom.

"Who are you!"

Slocum said, "I'm a man with a message. And

the message is this: Stay away from Cotilda
Murphy and her girls, from now on. She's not
alone anymore, and she's not afraid. You come
after her and you come after me."

Slocum's own eyes were cold and hard.

"I've got a list of my own in my head, Burns,
and now you're on it."

Turning, he rode off, not looking back as
Burns fumed.

"I'll see you again, Slocum!" he called. "And
when I do, you'll wish you'd never heard my
name!"

7

Slocum arrived back at Cotilda Murphy's camp to find a circuslike atmosphere. It seemed that most of the town of Parker was now playing, or *trying* to play, the game of baseball.

Everywhere Slocum looked, one of Cotilda's girls, dressed in her baggy uniform, was holding a seminar for groups of Parker citizens. The crack of bats hitting balls filled the air, and once more Slocum was greeted by the arc of a white sphere sailing closely over his head.

Slocum looked for Cotilda but couldn't locate her in the mayhem—but La Vonda was plainly visible, her tall frame swinging like a mighty machine as she hammered ball after ball high into the sky, where a distant group of older men ran feebly in chase.

"You see?" she said to the ten-year-old youngster watching her hit. "All you gotta do is hit it square!"

The youngster shuffled his feet and said, "I guess so . . ."

"Hey, La Vonda," Slocum said.

She turned her bright smile on him. "Why, Slocum, you old dog!" Her eyes suddenly darkened. "You been out to see Rafer Burns?"

Slocum nodded. "Saw your boyfriend, too. Pokey's all right, but I'm afraid one of Burns's men has met his reward."

The color drained from La Vonda's face.

"Didn't I tell you about Burns? He'll go for you now for sure."

Slocum said, "Is that such a bad thing?"

La Vonda said, "Which one of 'em did you get?"

"Fellow name of Curt."

"Heck, he was nearly as mean as Burns himself. What happened?"

Slocum told her the story of Curt sneaking up on him, and she nodded.

"Sounds just like the snake. I guess you done the right thing after all, Slocum. They would have left you out there in the desert for prairie dog meat."

"That's about what I figured. This fellow Burns doesn't seem to like any hint of opposition at all."

"Now you've got him pegged," La Vonda said.

The youngster was tugging at her sleeve.

"Hit it again, lady!"

"I guess I'll be moving along," Slocum said. "If you see Cotilda, tell her I went into Parker to talk to the sheriff."

La Vonda nodded, then smiled. "You said you saw Pokey?"

Slocum nodded. "They were giving him a hard time when I got there. Burns and two other fellows, named Fontaine and 'Corporal,' were holding a snake over him just for fun. It didn't look like Pokey thought it was fun. They treat him like that all the time, La Vonda?"

"Yes."

Slocum shook his head. "Didn't look right to me."

La Vonda's eyes burned with hate. "If they ever harm that man, I'll do 'em all in myself."

Slocum said, "If you care for that man, La Vonda, you'd better think about getting him away from that bunch."

"Don't I know you're right, Slocum."

"Hey, lady!" the youngster said impatiently.

Slocum tipped his hat. "Be seeing you, La Vonda. We'll take care of this Burns fellow yet."

"Oh, heck, Slocum, I hope you know what you're doing."

"So do I," Slocum said, smiling slightly, and

he rode off, leaving La Vonda to go back to hitting long, high arcing baseballs into the blue sky.

Parker, Texas, was nearly a ghost town when Slocum rode into it.

He figured in a few years it really *would* be a ghost town—just like all the other nameless towns Slocum had ridden through lately. As the railroads went through, as the stage lines died out and the Indians were pushed farther into their reservations, or in some cases right out of the territories and states altogether, as the land became safe for white settlers who liked to be safe—well, places like Parker, founded as an outpost satellite of Fort Worth, by people who for some reason or other didn't want to live in Fort Worth, fed by the stagecoaches that no longer ran, would dry up and blow away.

Slocum tied his Appaloosa to the hitching post outside the sheriff's office, knocked, and, after hearing a gruff reply that sounded like "Come in," opened the door and entered.

Inside it was hot and stuffy, with the windows shut to keep the dust out, no doubt.

A man Slocum had not seen out at the ball field, trim and serious-looking, with a mustache as florid as Rafer Burns's was neat, sat eyeing Slocum with his feet up on his desk.

"Help you, stranger?" he said, not entirely in a friendly manner.

"You're the sheriff?"

"That's what it says on my contract. You got a beef about all that ball playing on the edge of town?"

Slocum shook his head and smiled, trying to act friendly.

"Not at all. In a way, I'm hooked up with them. I just wanted you to be aware of a small bunch of troublemakers that seem to follow that ladies' baseball team around."

The sheriff showed no interest.

"So?"

"I think they may cause a bit of trouble for you and your town, Sheriff."

"That so?" the sheriff said.

He unwound his long legs from the top of the desk and set them firmly down on the floor.

When he stood, he towered over Slocum by nearly six inches.

The sheriff brought his face close to Slocum's; close enough so that Slocum could smell the chaw of tobacco he'd been chewing recently, along with his bad breath.

"And your name is . . . ?" the sheriff said, squinting his eyes close to Slocum's face.

Slocum took a step back, to get away from the man's offensive manner as well as his breath.

"Name's John Slocum. And yours?"

The sheriff put his thumbs in his gunbelt and said, "Sheriff Riley."

"Well, Sheriff Riley, like I said—"

"I *heard* what you said, Slocum. And I figure I know what you're talking about. As a matter of fact, fellow name of Burns was in here last evening, and we had a right nice chat. Pleasant fellow he was."

Slocum said, "He's not as pleasant as he sounds—"

Anger flared on Riley's face. "Don't be telling me my business, Mr. Slocum. Truth is, this fellow Burns let me in on a little secret, which is that your lady friends out there may be pulling a little bit of a scam with this so-called baseball game of theirs. This Burns fellow has been on to them for quite a while, and he's figuring on letting me in on breaking their little scam up."

"Sheriff," Slocum said reasonably, "if you'd just let me tell you—"

Riley thrust a pointing finger at the door. "Get out, Slocum, and don't come back again. I told you I know all I need to know."

Abruptly, he sat down, put his boots back up on his desk, pulled a large chaw of tobacco from a draw, and slipped it inside his cheek.

Slocum was not surprised to see that when he opened his mouth, there were many teeth missing.

"Out, Slocum," Sheriff Riley said, and pointed again at the door. As Slocum opened the door, leaving the oppressive, hot office behind, he heard Riley spit tobacco juice and seem to chuckle.

8

Riding back to Cotilda Murphy's camp, Slocum lit one of his treasured Havanas and tried to think.

There was more going on here than he knew about. The way Sheriff Riley had acted was strange to say the least. Slocum had known plenty of lawmen who were fools; he had also known more than a few who were crooks, and Riley immediately presented himself for that category.

It was obvious that Burns had already both bribed and charmed the lawman, so there was no way that Slocum could rely on the sheriff of Parker for help.

Which was fine with Slocum—hell, who'd

want a man with breath like that on his side, anyway?

Laughing to himself, Slocum rode on.

When Slocum got back to the baseball field, a full-fledged game seemed to be under way.

The crowd had spread itself down each of the sidelines of the field, while on the field itself Cotilda's Fort Worth 'Niners were playing, with a makeshift team from the town of Parker batting.

As Slocum rode up, a dignified-looking man was standing at the home base, removing his coat jacket and folding it neatly beside him. Under the jacket he wore red suspenders and a pressed shirt.

"Come on, Mayor, we ain't got all day!" someone shouted from the crowd.

There was a general guffaw, and the mayor stood primly.

"We got all day if I say so!" he shouted back, shaking his fist.

"Aw, just wait till the next election!" someone else shouted. "Then *you'll* be waiting all day!"

The entire crowd hooted, and the mayor suddenly snatched his coat up and stalked off.

La Vonda, who was pitching, had stood patiently on the mound, hands on her hips, but now she said, "Hey, get somebody up there to bat!"

Unwilling to upstage the mayor, the rest of

the Parker team shuffled their feet and looked at the ground.

Spying Slocum, La Vonda shouted, "Hey, Slocum, get up there and bat!"

Smiling, Slocum shook his head, but now the crowed got into the act.

"Yeah, mister, get on up there and show us what you can do!"

"Bet you can't hit it, mister!"

"Get up there and try, cowboy!"

Off behind the crowed, on the other side of first base, Slocum spied Cotilda Murphy grinning at him.

"What's the matter, mister—you afraid?" another voice hooted from the gallery.

"Well, all right then," Slocum said.

Getting down from his Appaloosa, he rolled his sleeves up and marched to where a pile of baseball bats lay on the ground.

"Well, okay!" someone shouted.

"He's gonna hit!" another voice chimed in.

A general cheer went up.

Striding to the plate, Slocum pushed back his hat and looked out at La Vonda, who looked at him cheerfully from the mound.

"You ready, Slocum?" she asked.

"Give me your best throw," Slocum said, waving the bat over his head like a weapon.

La Vonda laughed. "Batting like that, it won't be easy to get you out at all, Slocum!"

Slocum gave her a determined, concentrating look.

"Try and get me out," he said.

She laughed. "All right then, Slocum."

She took a windup and threw a pitch, which was by Slocum almost before he saw it leave her hand.

"What the—"

La Vonda hooted a laugh. "Fast enough for you, Slocum?"

Slocum glanced over at Cotilda, who was laughing softly in the wildly cheering crowd.

"Come on, mister!" someone next to her shouted. "*Hit the ball!*"

Slocum turned back to face La Vonda.

"Throw another one, woman," he challenged.

Smiling, she shrugged, then wound up and pitched again.

This one Slocum saw, but as it reached the plate it dipped a good four inches under his swinging bat.

"Aw, heck, he ain't no good at all!" a voice from the crowd called, and now there were hoots and catcalls in with the cheers.

"One more, La Vonda," Slocum said, some of the game coming back to him now. There had been a fellow from Georgia in the Confederate Army who had pitching tricks like La Vonda's.

Slocum said to himself, I bet she'll throw that curving pitch again.

"Come on, La Vonda!" Slocum said, egging

the pitcher on, waving his bat around menacingly.

"Here it comes, Slocum!" she said, taking a huge windup and letting the ball fly.

Slocum waited, eye on the ball, and when he saw it dip like he had expected, he gave a mighty up-swooping swing and caught the pitch solidly.

With the crack of the bat, the crowd gave a mighty sigh, and then they began to cheer wildly as the ball sailed up and still up, heading for the most distant reaches of the outfield.

Slocum threw the bat aside and began to run the bases, turning to grin at La Vonda, who stood chagrined on the pitcher's mound, shaking her head in disbelief.

"I gave you my best pitch!" she said.

"And I hit it!" Slocum said, sweeping his hat from his head to wave it at the crowd as he ran.

"You're the best, mister!"

"We want you on our team!"

Slocum put his hat back firmly on his head.

As he reached home plate, the outfielders had barely reached his ball, and Slocum stood grinning back at La Vonda.

"There's your best pitch!" he hooted, pointing at the farthest dusty reaches of the field.

La Vonda only scowled at him.

The mayor had been waiting for Slocum, and now drew him aside.

"Would you consider playing for Parker's team, Mr. Slocum?" he asked.

Slocum scratched his chin. "Well, now, I don't know. I'd have to think about that—"

"Go ahead," a laughing voice said, and when Slocum turned around, he saw Cotilda grinning at him.

"You wouldn't mind?" Slocum said.

"Not at all," Cotilda said. "Like I told you, we like to make these games interesting."

The mayor, scratching his own chin, said, "We could . . . make it worth your while, Slocum. I think the payment could be . . . quite interesting."

A crowd had formed now, and men were clapping Slocum on the back.

"Nice work, mister!"

"Get him for our team, Mayor!"

"Good hitting, mister!"

The mayor cocked an eye at Slocum and winked.

"*Very* interesting, Slocum. You could leave here a fairly rich man . . ."

Slocum smiled. "Well, now, I'll certainly think about that, Mayor," he said, shaking the man's hand. "Okay if I let you know tomorrow?"

The mayor looked at him closely. "You won't be riding out on us, will you?"

Slocum looked at Cotilda and said, "Mayor,

I promise, I'm not going anywhere."

After the mayor and the crowd drifted away, Slocum stood facing Cotilda Murphy, who gazed up at him, smiling.

"Nice job of hitting, John," she said.

Slocum touched his hat. "Why, thank you, ma'am."

Her face was flushed, and she pushed herself up against him.

"You know, John, I was going to wait until tonight, but I don't think I can wait . . ."

Teasingly, Slocum feigned incomprehension.

"Why, Miss Cotilda, I'm afraid I don't know what you mean—"

"*This* is what I mean," Cotilda said, slipping her hand down inside his trousers and pressing against him tightly so no one could see.

In a moment her work began to have the desired effect, and Slocum found himself looking around embarassingly.

"Cotilda," he said, "perhaps we should find a place—"

Gazing up at him with a mixture of mischief and need, she purred, "Why, John, what's wrong with you? You want this to be a secret love?"

"It's just that—" Slocum said, true hardness beginning to assault his member.

She pressed even tighter against him.

"What's the matter with right here?" she cooed.

A woman and her husband passed right by at that moment, and Cotilda turned to smile at them politely as they noticed nothing, walking on their way.

Inside Slocum's trousers, Cotilda's expert fingers, even in their cramped working space, were producing amazing results.

"Cotilda, I don't think this would be a good place," Slocum said.

"Why not?" Cotilda cooed, giving Slocum's rigid cockhead a playful, loving squeeze which nearly made Slocum see stars in his head. "Don't you like what I'm doing?" Cotilda said.

"It's not that—"

Suddenly she laughed, turning back to look up into Slocum's eyes.

"I have a place in mind to finish this business," she said, and Slocum nearly sighed in relief.

9

Slipping her hand from inside his trousers, Cotilda led Slocum by the hand through the milling crowd, which Slocum negotiated by removing his hat from his head and holding it strategically over his middle.

"Nice batsmanship!" a portly man said, clapping Slocum heartily on the back, nearly making him drop the hat.

"Thanks," Slocum mumbled distractedly, as Cotilda laughed, leading him along.

They made it through the crowd, leaving the baseball-engrossed masses behind and heading into the desert.

"Where we going?" Slocum said.

Cotilda merely stopped, wheeled around, and

pressed herself against him, once again slipping her hand into his trousers, to reawaken his hardness while pressing a kiss on his lips.

"We'll be there soon," she said.

They walked until they had left the baseball field far behind.

"One of the girls found this this morning, while out looking around," Cotilda said.

"Found what—?" Slocum began, but then he saw what she meant, as a square hole rose up out of the ground. It was the opening of an abandoned mine shaft.

"Someone from town told me the area around here is dotted with these mines," Cotilda said. "At one time they thought there was a copper lode in these parts, but it never panned out."

She yanked Slocum into the dark opening, and almost immediately began to pull his clothes off, as well as her own.

Pulling Slocum's trousers roughly down, she took his exposed cock in both her hands, knelt, and gently guided it into her mouth.

Coming up for air, she moaned, "I've been dreaming about this since last night . . ."

She went back to work, as Slocum stroked her hair, holding it in bunches as she took his rock-hard member deep into her mouth, sucking it right up to its tip before plunging her mouth down around it again.

Slocum began to feel the white juice build in his balls as the need in his love-gun wound tighter and tighter, toward eventual explosion—

"Oh, John!" she gasped suddenly, pulling her mouth from his dick and pressing him back on the cool ground to climb aboard him.

"John! Fill me!" she wailed, her cries echoing down the empty black tunnel of the mine as she dropped her open self down around his cock, drawing him deep into her wetly boiling recesses, her nether muscles massaging Slocum to even tighter hardness.

Grunting, Slocum pushed up against her, driving himself even deeper into her.

"Oh, John!" she screamed in ecstasy.

Straddling Slocum like a fine steed, Cotilda now began to buck wildly above him, driving her middle down the length of Slocum's love shaft and then pulling herself up its slick length almost to the tip before riding back down again. Her mouth opened in little huffs of pleasure and her head was thrown back as she moved with abandon on Slocum's love machine.

"Yes! Yes!" she breathed, and Slocum could feel her hot, wet innards grow ready to burst with orgasm.

"John, are you ready?" she begged.

"Any . . . time . . ." Slocum grunted, accompanying her wild buckings with his own well-timed thrusts.

"Now, John—*now!*"

And then she exploded around Slocum's

shaft, her entire middle convulsing in hard, rippling waves as wet juice billowed out of her.

And Slocum obliged by letting go himself now, his pump primed to readiness and now firing off hard, white shot after shot of cum, which seemed only to drive Cotilda to further heights of orgasm and pleasure.

"My God, John! My God!"

And then Slocum thrust his dick up as Cotilda drove herself mightily down, and the two of them exploded their mightiest effort together, steaming white juices slamming together like titanic ocean waves in the midst of a roiling, storm-drenched sea.

"John!" Cotilda screamed, her cry of abandon and joy echoing down the empty tunnel.

And now, spent, the seas calming, she collapsed down against Slocum's chest, feeling his spent hardness still within her, feeling their comingled juices trickling hotly down Slocum's cock and out of her hole, a sweet feeling.

"Oh, John," she said, resting her head softly on his chest, "that was wonderful."

Slocum stroked her hair and said, "You're welcome, ma'am."

Still sensing him within her, even as the juices were drying against her skin, she felt suddenly rejuvenated and raised herself on her hands to look mischievously into Slocum's face.

"Uh-oh," Slocum said, smiling.

"Once more, John," Cotilda cooed, and now Slocum felt himself growing rock hard inside her again.

"Or maybe twice," she said, beginning to move against him again.

After their loving, Slocum lay leisurely with his back against the tunnel wall, Cotilda beside him as they studied the afternoon desert outside the tunnel opening.

"I rode out to see Rafer Burns this morning," Slocum said, and for a moment he felt Cotilda stiffen beside him.

"There's one less of his gang to worry about now," Slocum said, and he told her the story of his attempted ambush and the shooting of the gang member named Curt.

"He had it coming," Cotilda said, eyes cold.

"But you don't think that'll stop Rafer, do you?" Slocum queried.

"Nothing will stop Rafer Burns," she said, and for a moment she pressed herself more snugly against Slocum.

"And it was stupid of you to ride out there," she said. "Because now you're on his list."

"That's just what I wanted," Slocum said. "Two minutes with the man told me all I need to know about him. Sooner or later I'm going to have it out with him. And I have a feeling it can only end one way, with me or him dead."

"Oh, John!" she cried, fearfully. "If anything happens to you . . ."

He turned to smile at her.

"I'm not planning on having it end that way," he said.

After a while they left the privacy of the tunnel and walked back to the ball field.

Slocum was surprised to see that only a few of the local townspeople remained—five men throwing a ball around in the outfield.

La Vonda met them, with a twinkle in her eye.

"Well, well," she said, smiling, "I was wondering if we'd ever see you two again."

Slocum nodded toward the men in the outfield. "Where'd everybody go?"

"Back to town," La Vonda said. "Tall fellow came riding out and told them all to leave. Said he was the sheriff." She nodded toward the outfield.

"He told that bunch, the best that were here, to stick around. Said there'd be more men coming out to finish the town's team."

Slocum and Cotilda looked at each other, and after a moment La Vonda caught on. "Burns and his men?" she said.

Slocum said, "That explains a lot. I'm sure the sheriff threw himself in with Burns. It would explain the way he treated me when I went in to see him today."

"You think they paid him off already?" La

Vonda said. "It wouldn't be the first time this happened."

Slocum said, "One way or another, Sheriff Riley is in Burns's pocket."

"What about those five out there?" Cotilda asked, businesslike.

"They're not bad," La Vonda said. "Three of 'em can hit, at least when I don't use the fancy stuff on them." She winked at Slocum.

"I saw your fancy stuff, and *I* hit it," Slocum said, smiling.

La Vonda hit him on the arm. "I've got better than that."

"What about fielding?" Cotilda asked, still serious.

"Well," La Vonda said, "they looked all right to me. Nothing special."

"Burns's man Fontaine will pitch, of course."

"Yeah," La Vonda said, and the smile disappeared from her face.

Seeing Slocum's questioning look, she added, "He's dirty. Throw at your head."

Slocum nodded.

"I'm just wondering," he said, "if they'll still insist on me playing on their team."

"We'll see," Cotilda said.

And then she grabbed Slocum's arm in a tight grip, because there, riding out of the late afternoon sun, were Rafer Burns and his men.

10

The smile on Rafer Burns's face was wide and friendly as he rode leisurely up, his men following behind.

"Afternoon, ladies!" Burns said politely, sweeping his hat from his head.

He looked dashing and handsome with his slicked-back hair and his pencil-thin mustache, but Slocum knew that underneath the manners he was all snake.

Rafer bowed his head slightly toward Slocum, his smile hardening.

"Mr. Slocum," he said.

His eyes stayed locked on Slocum's, as he spoke loudly.

"We had a funeral this afternoon, thanks to Mr. Slocum!" Rafer said. "It seems one of our merry band, the gentleman known as Curt, was drilled through the heart with a bullet fired by Mr. Slocum."

His cold eyes bore into Slocum murderously.

"We both know why that happened," Slocum said.

"Oh?" Burns said innocently. "The way I remember it, it was cold-blooded murder. In fact, I'm about to ride into town to have a talk with Sheriff Riley about it. I'm sure they have laws against cold-blooded murder in these parts."

"Talk all you want," Slocum said. "We both know what happened. And Pokey Johnson knows the truth."

"Pokey?" Rafer said, turning in his saddle to look at the sheepish man who rode behind him with his head down.

"Y-Yes, Mr. Burns?"

"Pokey, would you please tell Mr. Slocum what you saw him do this morning?"

Without looking up, Pokey mumbled something in a low voice that no one heard.

"Louder, please, Pokey," Burns ordered.

Glancing up briefly to give Slocum an embarrassed look, Pokey said in a low voice, "I saw Slocum kill Curt in cold b-blood."

La Vonda, shocked, said, "Pokey, how could you say that!"

Pokey looked at her pleadingly.

"Are you *sure* of what you saw, Pokey?" Burns said, and the way he said it made Pokey look up at him before looking away.

"Y-Yes, Mr. Burns. I'm sure."

La Vonda ran to Pokey and put her hand on his arm.

"Don't lie, Pokey!" she said.

"S-Sorry, Miss La Vonda," he said.

Rafer Burns, smiling, made a sweeping motion with his hat and put it back on his head. He turned his eyes to Cotilda, who shrank back.

"I'll be seeing you, Cotilda," he said, "after I finish my business in town. You might be interested to know that the kind people of Parker have decided to let us play with their baseball team on Sunday." His oily smile widened. "I trust we'll have a pleasant game."

He turned to his men and said coldly, "Let's go."

Burns and his men rode past.

Pokey Johnson, in the rear, looked quickly at La Vonda and then away.

In a few moments Burns and his men were gone.

"I can't believe my Pokey would lie like that!" La Vonda said.

"He'll do whatever Burns tells him to," Slocum said. "All I can hope is that the town of Parker's system of justice works the way it should."

Cotilda said, "John, you know you can't stay here! Sheriff Riley will railroad you into jail for sure! You said yourself he's in Burns's pocket!"

"Unfortunately, there's nothing I can do about it. Burns is counting on me hightailing it out of here. That's part of his plan."

Slocum looked at the settling dust from Rafer Burns's departure.

"But I'm a better poker player than he is," Slocum said.

Slocum enjoyed another good meal from La Vonda's hands before saddling up his Appaloosa as darkness was falling.

"Where are you going?" Cotilda said, with concern.

"Got to take another ride, is all," Slocum said.

Cotilda reached up to brush her fingers across his leg.

"I thought we'd . . . ," she said, smiling coyly.

Slocum smiled back. "There'll be plenty of time for that," he said. "This is work I've got to do. You remember you hired me to protect you, and that's what I've got to do."

"You'll be careful?" she said.

Slocum nodded. "Always am."

He spurred his Appaloosa, leaving her behind,

looking after him dolefully.

In a way, this was one of the things that Slocum had missed. Being in the hunt was an energizing thing, whether you were the hunter or the hunted.

Being both kept Slocum's reflexes doubly sharp.

He pulled a Havana from his pocket and lit it up, with a lucifer struck against his saddle.

The smoke was sweet, mixing with the cooling night. The sun was nearly below the horizon, and Slocum knew that with its departure the creatures of the night, hunters and hunted, would emerge. There were rattlers, and foraging coyotes, and the occasional bobcat looking for an unlucky and slow mule deer to prey on. In the morning, the turkey buzzards would feast on whatever was left of all these interesting interactions from the night.

Slocum knew that there were also human hunters and hunted who used the night.

He thought he knew Rafer Burns's mind, at least to the extent that he knew that Burns would not wait for Sheriff Riley to do his job. That would be Burns's backup plan. A man like Burns, half-predator animal, never left a job to someone else when he could do it himself. That was part of the thrill his sick mind obtained from his actions.

He would strike tonight, if he could.

But Slocum meant to be ready.

Pulling in another sweet pull of cigar smoke and blowing it out into the desert night, Slocum, hunter and hunted, rode on.

Their camp was fairly close nearby. They had moved it, but not very far; being a predator, Burns was like a lion and inherently lazy. They would have buried their companion Curt in a shallow rock grave, then moved their camp just far enough away not to have to watch the desert animals dig up the body.

There were two of them in camp. Slocum rode close enough to see by their firelight that they were Pokey Johnson and Fontaine, who had been left behind.

Fontaine, of course, was the baseball pitcher; apparently he was not as good at killing as Burns and the one Burns called Corporal.

But that didn't mean that Fontaine wasn't good at giving Pokey Johnson a hard time, since Fontaine was making poor Pokey sing very badly, while Fontaine hooted in mirth.

"Gosh-*dammit*, Pokey, that's the worst singing I've ever heard in my entire *life*! Boy, where did you learn to sing—a stable?"

Pokey stammered, "I-I t-told you, Mr. Fontaine, I n-never could sing worth a lick."

Fontaine howled. "Well, try it again! And try using a tune this time!"

"I-I'd rather not—"

Fontaine's voice became menacing. "Now, Pokey, you answer me this: Would you rather sing, or get beat?"

"I already t-told you, Mr. Fontaine, I-I'd rather sing."

"Then sing, dammit!"

Pokey took a deep breath and once more launched into a mournful cowboy tune:

> *"When the d-doggies are d-down*
> *For the night, outside t-town,*
> *And the c-cowboys have eaten their f-fill—"*

Taking a swig from a bottle, Fontaine held up his hand and began to laugh again.

"Gosh-*damn*! That's awful!"

"I-I've got to g-go to the toilet, Mr. Fontaine," Pokey said humbly.

"Then *go* then! Just don't sing while you're doing it!"

Fontaine took a drink and began to laugh wildly.

Pokey walked out into the desert darkness, and Slocum swung his Appaloosa in the man's general direction.

When Pokey had dropped his drawers to do his business, Slocum called to him.

"Hey, Pokey," he said.

Pokey's eyes went wide, and he nearly jumped out of his dropped trousers.

"W-who—?"

"It's me, Slocum. Finish your business and get over here."

"I d-don't think I should be talking to you—"

For emphasis, Slocum drew his Colt from his cross-draw holster and cocked it.

Slocum heard Pokey's piss stream increase in intensity.

"Be right there, Mr. S-Slocum," he said.

"That's more like it," Slocum said.

In a moment the man had finished and was looking up at Slocum sheepishly.

Slocum noticed a fresh bruise around one eye.

"Fontaine do that to you?" he asked.

"No, sir. Mr. Burns did. To teach me a lesson."

Pokey looked at the ground.

"What was the lesson, Pokey? That you should lie about me when Sheriff Riley comes to arrest me?"

"S-Something like that. Mr. Burns wanted to make sure I remembered."

Slocum made sure Pokey looked up to see his Colt.

"What if I told you you should tell the truth?"

Pokey began to quake. "Mr. Slocum, he'd kill me, he would! Mr. Burns would beat me, then kill me!"

"Why do you stay with him?"

Again, Pokey looked at the ground. "Because he wants me to."

"Don't you know that gal La Vonda is in love with you, Pokey? Don't you want the kind of life she could give you, away from Rafer Burns?"

When Pokey looked up, his stammer was gone, and his face was filled with longing.

"Know it? I dream about it every night, Mr. Slocum! It's all I ever dream about!"

"What if I told you the dream could come true?"

"How?"

Out by the camp fire, an increasingly drunk Lance Fontaine shouted, "Hey, Pokey, what's the matter with you? Get it stuck to your hand?"

Slocum whispered, "Tell him you're almost done."

Pokey shouted, "Be right there, Mr. Fontaine!"

Fontaine laughed.

"Hurry up! I want to hear another song!"

"All right, Mr. Fontaine!"

Fontaine laughed again.

"Gosh-*dammit*," he hooted to himself, "he's *awful*!"

Pokey turned his earnest eyes back to Slocum. "If I try to leave Burns, he'll kill me. Simple as that, Mr. Slocum."

Slocum said, "I'm going to take care of Burns."

Pokey shook his head. "If only you could . . ."

"Where is Burns now, Pokey?"

Pokey's stammer returned. "I r-really can't say, Mr. Slocum."

"He's out hunting for me, isn't he?"

Looking at the ground, Pokey nodded.

"Where?"

Pokey shook his head.

"Tell me, Pokey. For your dream."

Fighting himself, beginning to tremble, Pokey suddenly whispered, "He's camped outside Miss Cotilda's camp. He and Corporal are going to wait until midnight, then sneak in and shoot you dead. If that don't work, Sheriff Riley will arrest you tomorrow morning, they'll try you tomorrow afternoon, and hang you right after. It's all arranged."

"Thanks, Pokey. Go on back and sing for Fontaine, now. And keep dreaming. I got a feeling your dream's going to come true."

"If only it would . . ."

"Hey, Pokey!" Fontaine shouted, and now Johnson, giving Slocum a last mournful look, trudged back to the camp fire, while Slocum turned his Appaloosa back toward the baseball field.

11

It was harder to locate Burns and the Corporal than it had been to find their camp.

Slocum guessed that the Corporal had been a corporal in the Confederate Army, and possibly in a guerrilla brigade, because the two men had managed nearly to blend in with the night.

But Slocum had been a guerrilla, too, of course, and had learned from the best of them all—Quantrill himself.

And while his time with Quantrill and his murderous Raiders had nearly ended in Slocum losing his life—when Slocum drew the line and protested the outrage that Quantrill and his savages had perpetrated at Lawrence, Kansas—

his stint with the madman had also taught him nearly everything that had kept him alive all these years hence.

He had learned how to shoot his Colt with Quantrill.

And he had learned how to blend in anywhere—

And find anyone else who was blending in.

But Corporal and Burns were good, and Slocum was beginning to worry that perhaps the two badmen had already made their raid on Cotilda Murphy's camp when he came across them, not fifty yards off and fifty yards from the camp, outlined against the faint night.

Far off to the right, Slocum spied their tied horses, and he quietly made his way to that spot.

He untied the mounts from their Joshua tree and, quietly as possible, drove them off into the night.

Now Burns and his man would be on foot for the remainder of the evening.

Returning to his original spot, Slocum tied his own Appaloosa, checked his Colt in the dark before replacing it in its holster, and slid his Winchester rifle from its scabbard.

He crept forward in the darkness, toward the spot where the two men had been.

Their outlines were gone now.

Cursing silently, Slocum crouched, waiting for them to reappear.

Suddenly there was slight movement behind and to his left, and as Slocum reacted by swinging his Winchester around, a burly figure rushed at him in the dark.

Slocum was knocked back onto the desert floor, his Winchester flying out of his grip.

"So, Slocum!" a voice spat, "you made it easy for us!"

In the faint light of night, Slocum looked up into the raging face of the Corporal, who now raised his fist and brought it down in a strong arc at Slocum's face.

Slocum had been in this kind of fight before. But now, as he twisted his head to the side and pushed the other man's balance askew, a blazing shot split the night.

Desert sand was kicked up not two inches from Slocum's face.

"Burns, what the hell you doing!" Corporal yelled in outrage. "You nearly hit me!"

In the night, a soft laugh sounded.

"Came closer to Mr. Slocum, I think."

But now Corporal's attention was taken by Slocum, who threw the man aside and lay locked in the dust with him.

Slocum's fist found a good target, and he landed a punch in the man's face.

With an *oomph* of surprise, Corporal responded with a blunted punch of his own, and he and Slocum traded advantageous positions as they writhed on the dusty desert floor.

Again a shot sounded.

"Burns, cut it . . . out!" Corporal shouted, his breath labored from his efforts with Slocum.

Suddenly Slocum and Corporal were pushed apart, and the two men now rose into low crouches, circling each other like close wrestlers.

Another shot spit the sand between them, as Rafer Burns laughed.

"Burns, you're crazy!"

Trying to split his attention between Slocum and Burns, Corporal suddenly uttered a vicious oath and slid a long Bowie knife out of a sheath at his side.

"I'll finish this quick," he spat, and dove at Slocum, who evaded the blade and landed a mighty blow to Corporal's face.

"You should never rush anything, Corporal," Slocum said solemnly, seeking to land a second blow before finding his arm blocked as Corporal sought to undercut with the blade in his other hand.

Slocum barely avoided the cut before catching the bladed hand at the wrist and gripping it there.

The two men fell to the ground, grunting.

Rolling in the dust, Slocum sought to force the blade toward the other man's middle, but found that Corporal's strength was beginning to do the same thing to him.

Somewhere close by, Slocum heard the cock

of a gun and knew that Burns was about to fire off another shot.

Holding Corporal's hand in his tightest grip, he sought to stabilize their position for a moment, and did so.

The two men were locked frozen on the ground, Slocum on top of Corporal.

Then, with a mighty and abrupt move, Slocum reversed their positions, throwing himself to the ground and pulling his opponent over with him, even as the shot that Slocum had expected Burns to pull off split the night.

On top of him, Corporal went suddenly stiff.

"Goddammit, Burns . . . ," he said, and then he went slack in Slocum's grip, and fell over.

In the night, Rafer Burns laughed.

"Burns!" Slocum shouted, "You shot your own man!"

Burns continued to laugh.

"Yes," he said, "it seems I did."

Slocum scrambled away from the dead man's body, as another and then another shot smacked the desert floor near him.

"Your time is coming, Slocum!" Burns laughed.

Two more bullets ate the desert in front of him, their burning lines just inches from Slocum's retreating body.

"In fact," the badman shouted, "I think it's here!"

Slocum had backed himself against a stunted

cottonwood, and as he hit the tree, he heard Burns cock his weapon, preparing to make the death shot.

There was only a click.

"Damn!" Burns shouted.

Now, quickly, Slocum drew his Colt from its cross-draw holster and fired off a shot.

But Burns had melted into the night.

Slocum's reflexes became those of a cat. He waited, and watched, and nearly tasted the air to see if Rafer Burns was still within firing distance.

Slocum sensed nothing.

No movement, no smell, no whiff of the desperado at all.

"Gone," Slocum spat.

After satisfying himself that Burns was no longer in the immediate area, he went to the spot where the shots had come from and searched the ground.

He found his own Winchester, now empty of ammunition.

"So . . ."

The barrel was hot, and the smell of spent bullets permeated it like a second skin.

This had been the weapon that Burns had fired.

"So . . . ," Slocum said again, walking back to his Appaloosa, immediately slipping into the hunter's mode again, knowing that if he did not find Rafer Burns this night and settle the score immediately, he would be in even bigger trouble than he had been.

Burns was crazy, all right.

Crazy like a fox.

He had been laughing for a reason.

Slocum mounted and rode, a new, grim look now on his face, because now he was fighting for his very life.

12

But Rafer Burns had melted into the night.

Even without his horse, and without the companion he had murdered in cold blood—even with Slocum tracking him, Burns was nowhere to be found.

He might just as well have burrowed into the desert itself, or vaporized into the air.

Slocum searched every inch of the immediate area, but the man was not to be found. By that time, Cotilda Murphy's camp, awakened by the shots and commotion, had come out to investigate, but even with their help, there was no trace.

It was La Vonda who finally solved the mystery.

"One of our packhorses is missing," she reported, standing in the desert with the others in her robe.

"He went into the camp," Slocum said.

Cotilda, still bleary-eyed from sleep, said, "I'll mount up and help you look for him. Maybe we can get him on horse rustling."

"I doubt it," Slocum said. "He's too smart for that. He'll ditch the horse before we find it."

He wheeled around and said, "I'd better go alone. None of you are ready."

"The hell we're not," La Vonda said. Cinching her robe tighter, she ran to retrieve one of the saddled horses and appeared a moment later, ready to ride.

"That's my man out there with that devil, and I'm going with you, Slocum," she said.

"Then let's go," Slocum said, and the two of them kicked their mounts and rode out.

Slocum had a feeling their search would be futile.

They picked up the trail of the stolen horse easily enough, but the horse itself appeared not long after, grazing contentedly near a stand of Joshua trees, without a mark on it or any other sign that it had been stolen.

For all they could prove, the mount had wandered out of camp by itself.

"Damn," Slocum said.

As La Vonda stayed in the saddle and kept a lookout, Slocum studied the immediate area, but found no sign of human footprints, until he widened his search some fifty yards, where a pair of man's bootprints became visible.

Also at that spot were horse tracks, and Slocum would have bet his last gold piece that Rafer Burns had come across one of the horses Slocum had shooed away and ridden off on that.

He returned to La Vonda, flustered.

"Nothing to do but follow these tracks—but I bet they lead back to Burns's original camp, which will be empty now."

"Cotilda and I keep telling you he's a lucky devil, but you just won't believe us, Slocum," La Vonda said. Anger entered her face. "If he's done anything to my Pokey, no amount of luck in the world will save him."

"Best we move on," Slocum said, though he believed every word that she said.

They followed the tracks, which was slow work, with Slocum climbing down to study the dark ground periodically. But they were met with a surprise when their final destination turned out to be not the burned-out campground Slocum had visited hours before, but another of the abandoned mine entrances that dotted the landscape around Parker, Texas.

"What the—" Slocum said, his brow furrowing.

He drew his Colt, dismounted, and approached the dark opening.

"Let me come, too!" La Vonda whispered fiercely.

Slocum waved her quiet. "Stay here, and cover my back. There's no use two of us going in there."

"You might need help!"

"You can give me more help out here. If anything bad happens, ride back like the wind to Cotilda and tell her to get the mayor of Parker and a group of men he trusts out here. Forget Sheriff Riley—he's already in Burns's pocket."

Slocum's face became even more concentrated as he gazed at the mine entrance.

"I've got a chilly feeling there's more going on here than just a bettor's baseball game . . ."

"Slocum!" La Vonda whispered, as Slocum turned resolutely toward the yawning square mouth of the mine's opening.

Slocum looked back at her.

"Be careful!" she said.

Slocum nodded, and turned back to his mission.

13

A darkness deeper than night enfolded Slocum as he stepped into the mine opening.

This was no lover's nest. Slocum smelled evil in here, something far more sinister than anything he or Cotilda or La Vonda had thought Rafer Burns had in mind.

Burns was at the bottom of this, also, but this mystery went far deeper than a desperado's dogging of a woman while he skimmed from her winnings.

Standing perfectly still, Slocum listened for the sound of Burns, or one of his men, still in residence in the tunnel.

But there was only the sound of ominous silence.

Slocum returned quickly to the mine opening.

"Find anything?" La Vonda said hopefully.

"Way too dark in there. And there's something I should have done first."

Slocum studied the area around the shaft's mouth and found what he was looking for in a few minutes.

He pointed east.

"Burns rode out that way, after coming here. Either he left something here, which I doubt, or he came to get something he was afraid of us finding. The second choice is my choice."

La Vonda said, "What could he possibly have been hiding here?"

Slocum shook his head.

"At this point, I have no idea. But from the way you talk about Burns, I wouldn't put anything past him."

Slocum holstered his Colt and began to search the ground for material to make a torch, then he stumbled on a half-burned-out one, which had been tossed aside.

"Looks like I get to use Burns's own torch to search his hiding place," Slocum said.

Without another word, he walked back into the mine shaft, deep enough so that his striking a lucifer could not be seen from the outside.

He pulled the stick match across his boot heel, was blinded momentarily by the bright glare, then lit the torch.

Instantly the mine shaft became lit as if by daylight.

Glancing back toward the shaft opening, Slocum saw nothing of interest, so he moved deeper into the shaft, noting its gradual slant downward.

As cool as the desert night had been, it was much cooler here in the bowels of the desert earth.

A shiver ran through Slocum, but it was not entirely from the sudden chill.

Something had been hidden here that was, as Slocum had sensed on first walking in, truly evil.

But Slocum found nothing.

The deeper he moved into the shaft, the less that sense of evil persisted.

You went past it, he told himself.

Stopped abruptly, he doubled back, holding the torch out in front of him now to study the walls and floor.

He nearly walked by it before he discovered what he was looking for.

There, to his right, about chest height, a deep niche, a slit almost, had been carved out of the wall.

Just deep and wide enough to hold a cache of papers.

Slocum went closer, studying the opening with the light.

Slowly, he held his free hand out to reach into the opening.

There was a sudden hissing sound from within, and Slocum jumped back, pulling his hand away as a coiled rattler came into the cone of his torch's light and sought to strike at his retreating hand!

Shouting, Slocum drew his fingers away even as the viper struck, fangs glistening.

Missing Slocum with its strike, the snake dropped from the hole to the floor, where Slocum crushed its head with the heel of his boot.

"Slocum, you all right?"

Slocum's breath steadied, and he shouted back, "Yes! It seems Rafer Burns left a little present for me, but it didn't do its job!"

"Be careful, Slocum!"

"I will," Slocum said, as much to himself as to La Vonda as he now searched the mine-shaft floor for a stick and, finding one long enough, poked it into the niche to root out anything else that might be hiding within.

There were no more snakes, but Slocum heard the crackle of a struck piece of paper, deep within the opening.

Working with the stick in one hand and the torch in the other, he worked the paper out of its hiding place, pulling it toward the opening.

Nearly out, it got stuck on something, and

now Slocum, recalling his recent battle with the snake, suppressed a shiver at putting his hand into the opening and did so, his straining fingers just able to pull at the caught paper.

It resisted for a moment, then moved into Slocum's hand.

As Slocum pulled it out, the thought occurred to him that the amount of force he had exerted to pull the paper free would have torn any ordinary document.

Even as he pulled the paper out and examined it, he already surmised by its feel that it was a piece of legal tender.

But Slocum was unprepared for the shock of finding in his hand a one thousand dollar bill in U.S. currency—the largest denomination that had ever been minted in the United States of America—and, as much as Slocum could tell, it was genuine.

La Vonda studied the bill in Slocum's hand and was dumbstruck herself.

"Is it real?" she asked.

"It sure looks real," Slocum said.

"My Lord, a fortune in one tidy little place," La Vonda marveled.

"The thing that truly boggles my mind," Slocum said, "is that this is the one Burns left behind."

La Vonda's eyes widened.

"How many do you think were in there?" she asked.

"That's a good question. A better one is, What were they doing there, and what are they for?"

La Vonda shook her head.

"There's no way that kind of money would be bet on a baseball game," she said.

Slocum nodded. "Then there's something else behind Rafer Burns's appearance here. Something far worse than harassing you ladies and throwing a few ringers into a betting man's baseball contest.

Still in awe, La Vonda held out her hand.

"Can I hold it for a second?" she asked.

Slocum smiled, and placed it in her palm. "Better yet, you get to guard it for now. With all the trouble I'm in already, it wouldn't look good for me to be carrying that kind of tender around."

La Vonda gulped at the responsibility. "You sure you want me to keep this?"

"Just don't tell anyone about it, for now. Do you have a good hiding place back at the camp?"

La Vonda thought a moment, then nodded. "Sure. There's a place in my cooking area I could stash it."

Slocum said, "Just don't put it in tomorrow's stew by mistake!"

La Vonda stared at the piece of paper in her

hand. "My Gosh," she said, "the things this little thing could buy."

Slocum became thoughtful again.

"That's what's got me truly worried about Rafer Burns," he said.

14

By the time Slocum and La Vonda got back to camp, the night was nearly spent. In a few short hours, the sun would be lipping the horizon, and a new day would begin, full of shouts and baseballs flying.

Yawning, Slocum left La Vonda safe within the camp and then turned his mount to make a camp of his own.

"Slocum, where you going?" La Vonda asked,

Slocum said, "I'll sleep a little way off, find a secluded spot. I don't think Rafer Burns'll come near here again tonight, and if I'm off a ways, maybe I can catch a little more shut-eye." He smiled. "If a baseball doesn't fly that far and hit me, that is," he said.

"See you later, Slocum."

"And La Vonda," Slocum added, remembering how quiet and brooding she'd been on the ride back.

"Yes?"

"I wouldn't worry too much about your man Pokey. Odds are he's got nothing to do with what Burns has planned."

"That's not what I'm worried about, Slocum," La Vonda said. "I'm worried about what Burns'll do to Pokey because he doesn't fit in with his plans."

"Well, we'll do what we can to keep him safe. And speaking of safe, you find a safe spot for that . . . commodity we found," Slocum said, lowering his voice.

It was La Vonda's turn to grin, as she pulled the thousand dollar bill from the front of her shirt and waved it at Slocum.

"Been safe all along," she said. "And I'll find an even safer spot for it now."

"See you later, La Vonda," Slocum said.

"Later it is, Slocum."

Slocum found himself a secluded spot more or less ringed by stunted cottonwoods about a hundred yards off, tied, checked, and fed his Appaloosa, unrolled his bedroll, and was asleep, his Colt beside him, almost before he lay his head down.

And seemingly a moment later, he was

awakened by the sound of someone creeping close.

Instantly Slocum gauged his situation and reacted—opening his eyes, pulling his Colt into his ready hand, and turning to face the intruder—

But it was Cotilda Murphy hovering over him, a startled look on her flushed face, as she froze in lowering her naked body over Slocum's.

"Why, Cotilda—" Slocum said, the adrenaline that had shot into his veins at the threat of danger now converting itself into another kind of instant energy.

Cotilda continued her descent, smiling.

"I just thought I'd surprise you, John," she said. "I told you before I'd see you tonight, and since the sun is about to rise, I thought it was about time to keep my promise, and . . ."

"And make something else rise first?" Slocum laughed, as she played with his trousers, freeing Slocum's already well-hardened member, which she stroked and then, lowering her mouth, began to lick voraciously.

Before long Slocum had shed himself of the rest of his clothes and kneeled before her as she finished with her mouth work, bringing Slocum's cock to the hardness of solid rock.

Raising her head, Cotilda said, "Why, I think you're ready for something else, John."

"Anything you say," Slocum agreed.

Gently, Slocum tasted one pert nipple and

then the other, watching them harden like tiny shells. His balls began to ache with building pressure.

But once again Cotilda was with him completely, turning herself around on hands and knees to take him in from behind, giving him a beautiful view of her firm little ass before opening herself below and taking Slocum's long member in her hand to guide it into her wet, hot interior. Slocum felt himself sliding tight and wet for a long time until he completely filled her up.

She gave a little grunt of pleasure, and now Slocum, up to his balls in a snug, hot, oiled vagina, so deep his belly was tight against her beautiful rump, began to move his love piston with the rhythm of her inside muscles, feeling Cotilda's whole body begin to respond to his movements as her mouth gave little gasps of pleasure.

She rocked with Slocum, moving back and forth on her hands and knees, her interior growing in anticipation of the explosion to come.

"John . . . soon!" she gasped.

"Whenever you're ready," Slocum grunted.

His cock was as hard as it had ever been, pulled along, it seemed, by her exquisite inner muscles, which were primed to near readiness and now sought to grab Slocum's dick in a caressing surrender much as Cotilda's mouth and then fingers had.

Slocum rode her like a bucking bronco, breaking with her every move, giving her every little thrust and push she needed to drive her to massive orgasm.

They bucked and thrust, Slocum driving and pulling into her hot hole, for what seemed like hours—until suddenly the sun was rising behind them.

"Very . . . soon!" Cotilda gasped, and then gave a little cry of ecstasy as the moment suddenly arrived, and she could hold out no longer.

"Now, John—give it to me now!"

Slocum was only too happy to oblige, having reached nearly his limit on holding back. His cock was like a steam engine stoked to maximum, ready to burst to pieces. And yet he found one tiny moment more of hardness, before the boiling in his balls erupted up the long, shooting ride of his cock and roared like hot, white steam out of his expanding, blowing cockhead and into her recesses—

"Oh!" Cotilda cried, pushed forward by the force of Slocum's discharge, which filled her even as her own muscles now clamped hotly around Slocum's dick, covering it in sweet, sliding creme of her own making, even as Slocum's second volley drove her forward yet again—

"Oh, John! Oh, God!"

Slocum slid his hands around her middle to

pull her close, even as a third and then fourth volley burst mightly forth, mixing with her own violent, white, sliding orgasms.

"Oh! Oh!" she cried in muffled ecstasy, as Slocum's grasping arms locked them together, even as their inner explosions sought to burst their middles apart, so great was their comingled orgasmic flood.

A river of white juice—hers and his—burst around the joint of their locked privates and began to run hotly down Cotilda's legs.

"Oh, John, that's incredible!" she panted, and just as it seemed the volleys would subside, Slocum found a final one rising from his love loins, as great as the rest, and now Cotilda, huffing in need and expectation, felt it coming, working her vagina into a final spasm—

And then it came! And Slocum's hands were nearly loosened from Cotilda as the blast commenced, and then his grip, now slippery with dripping cum, did loosen, and his dick was thrust nearly out of her hot white hole by the force of the ejection on their tight joining.

As a river of white, mixed cum roiled out of her, Slocum relaxed, his still-hard cock sliding effortlessly back into her loosening recesses.

Cotilda collapsed to the ground, Slocum still deep within her.

"John . . . ," she said, mightily exhausted, and in a moment she was asleep.

And Slocum, following her down, found himself resting on her back, even as her weakening muscles within still rolled and moved gently against his well-used member.

"Cotilda . . . ," Slocum said, yawning.

And in a moment he himself was asleep.

15

Slocum awoke, deep into the morning.

He was alone, but Cotilda had lovingly wrapped him in his bedroll.

Slocum pulled on his trousers, stood, stretched, and felt renewed. Judging by the sun, it seemed he had slept three or four hours, but he felt as if he had slept a hundred.

Having finished his dressing, he once again attended to his Appalossa and then approached camp, already loud with the sounds and sights of baseball.

La Vonda, seeing him coming, left the group of townspeople she was teaching how to pitch and came toward him.

"You look refreshed," she said, smiling.

Slocum nodded. "Feel fine," he said.

"Hungry?" La Vonda asked.

"As a horse," Slocum said.

"That's good, because I kept the griddle hot for you."

"Thanks," Slocum said, and before he knew it, he was decked out with another of La Vonda's excellent breakfasts.

As Slocum was finishing up, La Vonda said, "This is the day the locals choose their final team." A gleam came into her eyes. "Then the betting starts," she said, smiling.

"I imagine that's when things get interesting," Slocum said.

"You can believe that, Slocum," La Vonda said. "Don't get me wrong, we girls like to play baseball; but this is our living, and I've got to tell you, by the time we leave this little town, we'll have half their salaries in our pockets. Nothing fancy and nothing illegal—just plain old betting. And people love to bet against us. Figure their fine manly fellows should make short work of the little girls, and the town fathers all start crying for pride and all, and before you know it they've got themselves convinced they can't lose."

"And they always do?"

"They always do." Her face darkened. "Except when Rafer Burns is involved. Then things get nasty, and sometimes go the other way. What he'll do is, he'll use his men as the core of a team, then flesh it out with some big-ox locals who can hit the ball a ton. His men, ringers all, then do most of the work, win the game, and he takes half of what the town put up."

She frowned.

"Everybody's happy 'cept the Fort Worth 'Niners. When that happens, we come away with nothing but the memory of the smile on Rafer Burns's face."

Slocum looked out over the field and spied Cotilda Murphy off at the far end.

"Think I'll take a walk," Slocum said. Slyly, he added, "To get rid of that heavy feeling in my stomach, of course."

La Vonda smacked his arm.

"John Slocum, you know my cooking's about the best you've ever had."

Slocum shrugged. "It ain't on the bad side, I guess."

A faraway look had come into La Vonda's eyes. "If only I could cook like that for Pokey Johnson someday . . ."

Slocum said, "You will, La Vonda. Just hold on."

La Vonda brightened with a mischievous grin of her own. "Like you've been holding on to Miss Murphy?" she asked.

Slocum just smiled and walked off.

He found Cotilda setting up a table near the left-field side of the baseball diamond, and lining up markers where the line for betting would form.

"Expecting a crowd tomorrow?" Slocum said.

Cotilda smiled.

"Hello, John," she said. "And never mind tomorrow; the betting starts today. By afternoon you won't be able to get near this table, and by tomorrow morning they'll be fighting each other to lay their money down."

"You sure your girls are ready to play?"

Cotilda snorted. "You kidding? They're always ready. And they always win." Her face clouded.

Slocum said, "I wouldn't worry much about Rafer Burns," Slocum said. "If he's a smart man, he'll stay away. And he's only got himself and that pitcher fellow, Fontaine, left to play, anyway."

"He'll be here," Cotilda said with certainty. She looked at Slocum gravely. "And La Vonda told me about what you found last night."

She took Slocum's arm and looked up into his eyes with concern.

"I'm afraid he's got something bad planned, John."

Slocum nodded and suddenly spied the mayor making his way toward the field.

"Just the man I wanted to see," Slocum said. "I'll see you later, Cotilda."

Cotilda continued to hold his arm.

"I hope so, John . . . ," she said passionately.

Slocum caught the mayor as he was heading toward the betting table, a wad of small bills clutched in his hand. Behind him a line of eager bettors was already forming.

"Mayor, I need to speak with you," Slocum said.

The mayor, distracted, said, "Yes, yes."

He looked at Slocum closely, then smiled. "Why, aren't you the young man who's going to play for our team tomorrow?"

Slocum said, "I sure hope to, Mayor."

"Wonderfu!"

"Mayor," Slocum said, "I need to ask you a question. Has Sheriff Riley had any visitors lately? From out of town?"

The mayor frowned. "Well, there was that fellow Burns, of course."

"Anyone else?"

The mayor rubbed his chin, then brightened in remembrance.

"Why, yes! There were some Mexican gentlemen, also. The same day Mr. Burns was in town. I asked Sheriff Riley what it was all about, but he just said it was some sort of business deal Mr. Burns was involved in. Had nothing to do with Parker in the least."

The mayor looked beyond Slocum to the betting table, where he had now lost his bid to be first in line as Cotilda began to make book with a swelling number of citizens.

"Mr. Slocum, I really should be going . . ."

"You've told me all I need to know," Slocum said.

The mayor had moved past Slocum toward the betting table when a booming voice called out, "Mayor Drucker, hold that man!"

Slocum and the startled mayor turned around to see Sheriff Riley riding toward them. Behind him on horseback was Rafer Burns, followed by Fontaine and Pokey Johnson.

Riley pulled up next to the mayor. "Sir," he said, "you've done an excellent job in apprehending this man."

Drucker, confused, said, "I don't understand . . ."

But Sheriff Riley was already off his horse, his sidearm drawn as he marched toward Slocum.

Behind him, Rafer Burns smiled evilly.

Riley grabbed Slocum, turned him around, and began to tie his hands behind his back.

"John Slocum," he said grimly, "you're under arrest for the murders of Curt Bateman and Corporal James Carpenter, in cold blood."

The crowd gasped, and Cotilda Murphy, sitting at her betting table, lost all color in her face.

16

In a flash, Slocum had been bound, his Colt pulled from its holster, and he stood before Rafer Burns and his henchmen.

Sheriff Riley said, "Mr. Burns, is this the man who shot your friends?"

Burns nodded. "That's him, Sheriff. Shot them in cold blood. Corporal Carpenter, who was a hero in the war, he shot in the back."

"Is this true?" Mayor Drucker said, astounded.

Sheriff Riley nodded. "We've got the bodies in town. Carpenter was definitely shot in the back."

Slocum said, "And Rafer Burns did the shooting."

Burns, eying Slocum with disdain, said, "I suggest you check Mr. Slocum's Winchester rifle. That was the weapon he used to shoot Carpenter."

Riley said, "I'm going to have to take you into town, Slocum." He turned to the mayor.

"Looks like we're going to have a trial. And I think it should be a quick one, so as not to spoil tomorrow's festivities . . ."

Mayor Drucker said, "Oh, dear. And it's been a while since we've had a hanging in Parker . . ."

Word of Slocum's arrest had already spread, and a crowd was forming. From the middle of it stepped Cotilda Murphy and La Vonda.

La Vonda looked at Pokey Johnson sitting unhappily on his mount and said, "Pokey, tell them what really happened!"

Pokey said nothing, and Slocum caught the slight smile that formed on Rafer Burns's lips.

"John!" Cotilda said, "I won't let them do this to you!"

Someone had fetched Slocum's Appaloosa, and after Sheriff Riley pulled Slocum's Winchester from its scabbard, Slocum was hoisted up onto the horse for the ride into town.

He looked down at Cotilda.

"Don't worry," he said.

Mayor Drucker, still looking disturbed, said, "Oh, dear, and he was such a good ball player,

too. Now I don't know what we're going to
do . . ."

Rafer Burns said, "Don't worry, Mr. Mayor.
I think I can help you on that score."

And as Slocum's Appaloosa had been led
away, already Rafer Burns had his arm around
Mayor Drucker's shoulder, and a new team for
Parker, Texas, was forming around Burns as a
quick trial and possibly a quick noose waited
for John Slocum.

Within a half-hour Slocum had been thrown
into a jail cell. Sheriff Riley himself locked
him in after untying him, stopping just long
enough by the bars to look down at Slocum and
say, "I'll wager that by tomorrow morning your
neck'll be longer than your luck, Slocum." He
grinned. "And speaking of luck, I think I'll go
on back to the ball field and lay my money
down on Rafer Burns's team to win tomorrow."

"We'll see whose luck runs out, Riley,"
Slocum said.

Riley laughed and walked out, rattling his
keys.

From the back window of the cell, Slocum
could look out on the outskirts of town, and
he was treated to a pretty fair view of the ball
field, which lay beyond.

Already Burns had a team organized on the

field, while Cotilda's girls stood idly by, staring with disdain.

And, as Cotilda had predicted, the betting table was swamped with customers, nearly overrunning La Vonda, who now took wagers, with two of the other girls helping in the rush.

Cotilda Murphy was nowhere in sight.

Not on the field, anyway—because now Slocum heard a commotion out front in the jail, out of his sight, and Cotilda Murphy's voice rose in argument with Sheriff Riley— before Cotilda herself appeared, rushing to the bars of Slocum's cell.

"John, are you all right?" she said with concern.

Slocum gave her a smile. "So far," he said. "Sounds like you gave the sheriff hell, though."

"He didn't want to let me in to see you," she said.

Slocum nodded over her shoulder, where Riley, almost but not quite out of sight, stood nearby, listening to their conversation.

Whispering, Slocum said, "This isn't a good time to talk. Come back after sundown, to the back of the cell."

He nodded his head toward the rear window.

"All right, John," she said. Louder, so that Riley could hear, she added, "Please take care of yourself, John. I'll see you tomorrow."

"I'll do that, ma'am," Slocum said, loudly, and as Cotilda left, he winked at her.

Forming the words in a silent whisper, he said, "Tonight," and she nodded, smiling back at him.

The next hours seemed about as long as any that Slocum had ever waited. When Sheriff Riley wasn't walking back to jeer at him—which was often enough—Slocum was at the back cell window, watching Rafer Burns and his sidekick Fontaine turn the rough-and-tumble fellows of Parker, Texas, into a real baseball team. By late afternoon the nine men that Burns had assembled looked as good as could be—certainly good enough to beat Cotilda Murphy's team.

The betting table seemed to reflect this fact—since the lines only swelled as the day wore on toward sundown.

As things were now, Cotilda Murphy stood to lose her baseball game and her stake—and Slocum stood to lose his life.

That wasn't the kind of wagering Slocum was fond of participating in.

Finally, Slocum found he didn't like the view of the ball field any longer—so he sat down with his back to the jail cell wall, pulled his hat over his eyes, and began to think.

The way out of this mess was to figure out what Rafer Burns really had in mind: what that one thousand dollar bill, and all the other thousand dollar bills that went with it, were for.

They had been payment to Burns for something. But what? With a little thought, it was clear to Slocum that the Mexicans who had visited Burns in Sheriff Riley's presence had been the payers—but what had they been paying for?

Whatever it was, it would probably be transported back to Mexico—which meant that the Mexicans were still in the area, hiding out somewhere.

But what could they be buying in Parker, Texas, that would cost that kind of money?

At first Slocum was sure it must have something to do with the played-out mines that dotted the landscape in those parts. Maybe a secret strike of silver or even gold had been made, and Burns was throwing his lot in with Riley to steal it all.

But that didn't make sense—as far as Slocum knew, Burns had been following Cotilda Murphy and her gals around for some time, and anyway, how could a mining strike be kept secret for long?

And why transport the ore to Mexico?

There had to be some other sort of valuable freight in Parker, Texas . . .

And then, after a long time of thought, as the sun dropped below the bars of the back window of Slocum's cell, just as he was drifting off to sleep with thoughts of Cotilda Murphy on his mind, it came to him, and Slocum suddenly knew just how evil Rafer Burns really was.

He's worse than a snake, he thought.

Quickly Slocum began to form a plan in his head to thwart Rafer Burns's plans—

"Hey, Slocum!"

Slocum looked up from under his hat to see Sheriff Riley grinning at him.

"What is it, Riley?" Slocum asked.

"You hear that?" Riley said, cocking his head toward the front of the jail, where, from the street, came the sounds of banging hammers.

Slocum nodded. "I hear it."

"That's your gallows, Slocum!" Riley laughed. "I figured I might as well put the carpenters to work, so I told them to rig up your hanging box tonight! No sense wasting time, since you'll be swinging in it tomorrow!"

Grinning under his large mustache, Riley turned on his boot heels and walked back out front, laughing to himself.

Slocum stood, and, making sure that Riley was gone, he turned to the back window.

There, to his relief, was Cotilda, waiting in the new darkness below the window.

"John!"

Slocum put himself closer to the bars and smiled down at her. "Thanks for coming," he said.

"Can Sheriff Riley hear us?" Cotilda whispered.

"I doubt it," Slocum answered. "He's out front now."

"Good," she said. Her face became serious. "John, they're building a gallows out front. What can I do to help you?"

"Got a truckload of dynamite?" Slocum said jokingly. Then, in a more serious voice, he said, "There's something real important you've got to get done. Can you spare one of your girls for the job?"

Cotilda nodded. "I only need nine for the game tomorrow. I'll play myself. That'll leave one to spare."

"Good," Slocum said. "She's got to make a long ride, so pick one who's good and fast on a horse. You know a lawman you can trust in Fort Worth?"

Cotilda said, "Yes. The marshal there is a good man."

"We're going to need him, and fast. I think I've figured out what Rafer Burns has in mind, and a federal marshal is just what we need to break up his plans. Sheriff Riley is in on the plot, too. We can't use the telegraph here because I'm sure Riley would find out about it. Your girl's got to get through."

"I'll make sure she does," Cotilda said. "But what does she tell the marshal to get him here?"

"Tell him there's a band of Mexican rustlers about to attack Parker, Texas, and that he's got to search the mine openings in the area and flush them out. I'm sure Rafer Burns has them hiding in one of the mines."

Cotilda looked up in surprise.

"Cattle rustlers? There aren't any cattle here . . ."

"It's not cattle they're rustling," Slocum said. His face had become grim. "It's that thousand dollar bill that finally put me on to it. That kind of money just doesn't change hands for very many things. One of the only things in this part of the world that could cost a thousand dollars is a white American woman."

All of the color had drained from Cotilda's face.

"You mean—"

Slocum nodded.

"I'll wager that Rafer Burns has another eight thousand dollar bills to match the one La Vonda and I found in that mine shaft. I'll also wager that after he sold your nine girls to the Mexicans, he was going to keep you for himself."

Rage had replaced shock on Cotilda's face. "But he can't—"

"Sure he can. We're not that far from the border; with Sheriff Riley's help, your girls would be over it and deep into Mexico before anyone even suspected. Burns's twin obsessions for a long time have been you and the money your girls generate—what better way to maximize the profits of both than to sell your girls off and finally have you for himself? You think he cares about what happens to La Vonda and the rest? If they were lucky, they'd end up as ladies of the night, earning back that thousand dollars and more in no time. Probably worse. You told me Burns was evil, and I have no trouble believing it, Cotilda."

"I'll kill him myself," Cotilda Murphy said, red rage filling her eyes.

"That's not the way to play this out," Slocum said. "You have to bring the federal marshal into it, and fast. In the meantime, you've got to go about your business here as if nothing is out of the ordinary. Remember," Slocum said, rubbing his hand across his own neck, "I've got my own troubles to worry about before we can get rid of Rafer Burns. I want that marshal here in case I don't get out of this mess with my neck intact."

Cotilda reached up to touch Slocum's face. "John, I won't let anything happen to you!"

"The way I see it, I've got to get Pokey Johnson to speak up at my trial. Without him, I'm sunk."

"I'll get La Vonda to find him," Cotilda said.

"Good—" Slocum began, but then there was a commotion behind him as Sheriff Riley approached the cell.

"Slocum! Get a good night's sleep!" Riley said, laughing. "It'll be your last!"

Slocum looked quickly down at Cotilda before turning away from the bars. "Go now, and do what I said!" he told her.

Cotilda nodded and moved off.

Slocum turned around as Riley reached his cell and stood before it, grinning, holding a dirty tin plate of cold food.

"Slocum," Riley said, putting the dish on the floor and pushing it into the cell with his boot toe, "you hungry?"

"Not hardly," Slocum said.

Riley laughed harder. "Well, I guess I wouldn't be hungry either if I were you. Being as the swallowing part of your anatomy is about to be altered."

He bent down, pulled the tin tray back, and slid it across the floor, into a far corner of the room. "Guess we'll let the ants eat it," he said.

"I haven't had my trial yet, Sheriff," Slocum said.

Riley sighed. "Guess you're right, Slocum. We have to get the trial part of it over with before I get to snap your neck with a rope."

He walked away, laughing. "Get a good night's sleep, Slocum! Hope you like the sounds of hammers!"

Slocum sat down with his back to the wall of the cell once more, and tried to sleep through the long night, with the sound in his ears of his own gallows being built, as he wondered if this would indeed be his last night, and if Rafer Burns would win more than just a baseball game come tomorrow.

17

"Slocum!" Sheriff Riley shouted. "Wake up!"

Slocum came awake with his stiff back against the wall of the cell.

Bright sunlight flooded the barred room. Slocum stood stiffly, rubbing at his aching back.

"What's the matter, Slocum? Little sore? We've got just the cure for that!"

Riley hooted, then rattled his keys, fitting one into the jail cell's lock and opening the door.

"Come on out then," Riley said. "Time for your meeting with justice."

Slocum glanced behind him out the back

window of the cell and saw that the baseball field was empty.

"No one out practicing baseball this morning, Slocum! They're all out front to see a hanging! Come on, now," Riley continued amiably, taking Slocum by the arm. "Can't keep the people waiting, can we? Reverend Gates even had church services extra early this morning, just so's we could get all the spectacle in!"

Gripping Slocum's arm tightly, Riley stopped to look malevolently into his face. "Being as it's the Sabbath and all," he said, "maybe you'd like to say a little prayer later before I put the noose around your neck?"

Slocum stared back evenly. "With what you've got yourself involved in, Riley, I'd be worried about my own neck if I were you."

Riley gave Slocum a vicious glare and shoved him out ahead into the front of the jail and then out into the street.

The area outside the jail had been converted into a makeshift outdoor courtroom, with the mayor sitting as judge on a high stool and a chair in front of the judge for Slocum to sit on.

The town of Parker had gathered around for the show; barstools had been carried out of the saloon for seating, but mostly the townsfolk sat on blankets with picnic lunches or stood lounging, as they would at any circus.

And off to the side stood a makeshift gallows, rope at the ready, looking all too serviceable.

"Our carpenters here in Parker do good work, don't you think, Slocum?" Riley said, laughing.

Slocum sat in his chair and waited for the festivities to begin.

The trial didn't take long. Mayor Drucker, unused to the role, merely sat nodding as Sheriff Riley, talking loudly and twirling his long mustache, paraded the evidence—Slocum's Colt and Winchester rifle—in front of the jury and showing them the bullet that had been dug out of Colonel Carpenter's back.

"You got anything to say, Slocum?" Riley said finally.

"Sure do," Slocum said, but Riley cut him off.

"Save it for the hangman," the lawman said, which produced chuckles and a few catcalls.

Slocum searched the crowd, finding Cotilda's worried face and Rafer Burns's smug grin but unable to locate La Vonda or Pokey Johnson.

Looks like you've had it, he said to himself.

"Is there anything else we should hear?" Mayor Drucker said, from his stool.

There was silence from the crowd.

"Well then, even though it's the Sabbath and all, I'm afraid we'll have to provide swift justice and . . ." The mayor looked at Sheriff Riley. "Are you sure we couldn't wait until tomorrow morning, say, sunup?"

Riley shook his head. "Got to be done today,

Mayor. God knows what other tricks Slocum has up his sleeve, and I'd hate to think about the danger to the citizens of Parker, never mind your reelection bid, if Slocum should escape."

The mayor sighed, and then looked sadly down at Slocum.

"I'm sorry, John Slocum," Mayor Drucker said, "but you'll have to hang, and hang now."

Cotilda Murphy cried out, and Sheriff Riley laughed.

"Come on, Slocum," he said, "time to die!"

Grabbing Slocum roughly by the arm, Riley led the prisoner toward the wooden gallows.

"Up you go, Slocum!" Riley taunted, shoving him toward the steps and forcing him up them one by one.

When they reached the top platform, Riley turned Slocum toward the crowd and slipped the expertly knotted noose around his neck. "Tied this one myself," Riley said and chuckled.

Slocum looked out over the crowd. Many of Parker's citizens wore the same entertained expressions they had worn on the baseball field, but Slocum noted the horrified, tearful face of Cotilda Murphy and, behind her, the smirking countenance of Rafer Burns.

"Anything to say, Slocum?" Riley said, stepping back to put his hand around the wooden lever that, when pulled, would remove the floor from under Slocum's feet and send him plunging to his neck-snapping demise.

Searching the crowd, Slocum didn't see the one face that could save him.

"Guess not," he said.

"That's just fine, then!" Riley said. "Why don't you just say good-bye!"

Sheriff Riley looked down at Mayor Drucker, still sitting on his stool. The mayor nodded morosely.

With a grin, Riley tightened his grip on the lever, as he started to pull it back—

Suddenly La Vonda's voice cried out from the rear of the crowd, "Wait!"

The mob parted, making room for La Vonda, who dragged a reluctant Pokey Johnson behind her like a rag doll.

"Now, you get up there and you tell what you're supposed to tell," La Vonda ordered him.

Without looking up, he nodded. "Yes, ma'am."

"Hey, Mayor!" Riley shouted. "Trial's over!"

Drucker looked up at Riley and said, "Not until I say so, Sheriff."

Mayor Drucker looked down at Pokey. "You have something to add to these proceedings?"

Pokey nodded sheepishly.

"Well, let's hear it, then."

La Vonda, sitting in front, caught Pokey's eye.

"Tell what you know, Pokey," she said encouragingly.

Pokey suddenly blurted out, "John Slocum didn't shoot Colonel Carpenter in the back. And he shot Curt in self-defense."

A wave of excitement went through the crowd, and Sheriff Riley looked very displeased.

"Is this true?" Mayor Drucker said. "You know these things for a fact?"

Looking at the ground, Pokey nodded. "Yessir."

"Do you know who *did* shoot Colonel Carpenter in the back, using Mr. Slocum's gun?"

Pokey glanced up and caught Rafer Burns glaring at him from the crowd. Suddenly he began to tremble. "N-N-no, sir."

"Are you sure?" Mayor Drucker asked.

Pokey's eyes were locked on Rafer Burns. "N-N-no, sir. I have no idea."

Mayor Drucker sighed. "Well, then, I have no choice but to let Mr. Slocum go. The evidence is stronger in his favor than against him. I hearby declare the killing of Curt as self-defense on Mr. Slocum's part, and the murder of Colonel Carpenter as unsolved at this time."

Drucker climbed down off his stool. "Sorry, folks, no hanging today. But we still have that baseball game to attend to!"

A general cheer went up, and Sheriff Riley glared murderously at John Slocum, his hand hesitating just a reluctant moment on the gallows lever before leaving it and removing Slocum's noose.

"This isn't over yet, Slocum," he said.

Slocum stared back coldly into the corrupt lawman's eyes.

"No, it isn't," he said.

18

Cotilda Murphy waited for Slocum as he left the gallows behind.

"Oh, John!" she cried, falling into his arms. "You're free!"

Grinning, Slocum rubbed his neck.

"But that was close," he said. Looking out over the dispersing crowd, which was moving back toward the ball field, Slocum frowned.

"Where's La Vonda, and Pokey Johnson?"

Cotilda said, "They're going to have to hide out. I'm afraid of what Rafer Burns will do to Pokey if he gets his hands on him." She smiled coyly up at Slocum. "I sent them to the abandoned mine we . . . used the other night," she said.

Slocum grinned. "I'm sure they'll be just fine, then."

Cotilda said, "La Vonda is a good woman, and she's going to make an honest man of Pokey."

Slocum continued to grin. "Sending them where you did will certainly give her a good start on the process," he said.

Turning serious, Slocum asked, "Did you get a rider off to Fort Worth, like I told you?"

Cotilda nodded. "She rode out last night. I'm sure Rafer Burns has no idea she's gone." She frowned. "It leaves me with a problem, though."

"What's that?"

"For the baseball game today, now I'm one short. Even including myself, I only have eight players."

"Can't you play with eight?"

Cotilda shook her head. "The wagering calls for nine players on a side." She snuggled up closer to Slocum. "I do have a solution, though."

Slocum looked down at her. "Oh?"

Cotilda said, "Since you're such a good ball player yourself, I thought you might play for my team."

Slocum shrugged. "Sure. I think it'd be interesting to play against Rafer Burns. Good a way as any to keep an eye on him while we wait for that marshal to get here. You'd better clear it with Mayor Drucker, though."

Cotilda smiled. "I will, John."

Seeing the mayor out in the crowd, she said, "I'll talk to him now. Then I'd better see to the wagering table, which seems to be mighty crowded at the moment." She gazed up into his eyes. "I'll see you later, then?"

"You can count on it."

"And tonight, after the game . . . ?"

Slocum grinned. "Anything you say."

Cotilda sighed happily. "I'm not half as worried as I was, John. Not with you around."

Slocum said, "We've still got to keep an eye on Rafer Burns. I don't think he's played his last card yet. In fact, I think I'll take a little walk now and see what he's up to."

"Till later, John," Cotilda said, still gazing into Slocum's eyes.

"Until later," Slocum said.

He knew the book was still open on Rafer Burns. Though Burns had failed in getting Slocum hanged, the badman no doubt had a backup plan. A man like Burns would always have a backup plan, and Slocum knew it was his own back that he had to watch from now on.

But there was Burns at the plate, a smile of seeming contentment on his face, teaching his chosen players from Parker, Texas, the finer points of the game out on the field.

His pitcher, Fontaine, was off in foul territory throwing a ball to a burly man acting as catcher, while Burns yelled encouragement to his players at their various positions.

"You there! Shopkeeper!" he shouted at a wiry but strong-looking young man playing center field. "Remember what I told you about the ball getting lost in the sun! Look to the side, and keep your eye on it until you catch it!"

With the bat in his hand, Burns hit a ball high and long that arced out to the man in center field, who did just what Burns had told him and caught the ball expertly.

"Excellent!" Burns cried. He pointed to the right fielder. "Now you!"

"Figuring on winning today, Burns?" Slocum said.

Burns ignored Slocum long enough to hit the ball high and far out to the right fielder; then he turned his mild gaze on Slocum.

"Why, Slocum. You're still here? I thought you would have found the environment around Parker, Texas, a little constricting after nearly losing your neck in it."

Slocum shook his head. "I'm here to stay, for now."

"Oh? Going to watch the big game today?"

"Figure I'll play in it," Slocum said. "Cotilda Murphy's asked me to fill in for one of her players."

Not blinking, Burns said, "Oh? I notice that Miss La Vonda is nowhere to be found. If Miss

Murphy herself played—and she is an excellent fielder, I understand—that would still make nine. Did another of her players take . . . ill?"

"Not really. Just off on an errand."

Slocum watched the badman's face, but there was no reaction in it.

Burns said, "So you'll be playing today?"

"That's right," Slocum said.

Smiling amiably, Burns turned to Fontaine, his pitcher, and said, "Did you hear that, Mr. Fontaine? Mr. Slocum here will be batting against you this afternoon!"

Fontaine grinned. "Is that so?" he said, and fired a pitch at his catcher, which nearly knocked the man down.

"Well, Mr. Slocum should know that I sometimes throw wildly—isn't that right, Mr. Burns?"

Having gotten the baseball back from his catcher, Fontaine fired another ball in, with even greater speed, and the catcher had to reach high and to the left for it, just about at head height.

The catcher threw his thin glove off and stood shaking his hand in protest.

"Owwww!"

Fontaine laughed, and Burns turned his amiable look back to Slocum.

"Be careful out there today, Mr. Slocum. And tell Miss Murphy that I'm saddened that one of her players took ill and can't play."

"I told you," Slocum said, staring into Burns's mild yet cold eyes, "that Cotilda's player had to go off on an errand. In fact, she had to ride into Fort Worth to fetch someone."

Burns's eyes remained impassive. "Whatever, Mr. Slocum. We'll see you on the ball field this afternoon."

Burns turned away from Slocum to point at his left fielder.

"Now you catch it!" he said, and when he hit a high, arcing ball to the man, it was caught flawlessly. "Excellent!"

Slocum turned away from Burns to see Cotilda running toward him, pale as a ghost.

Slocum caught her and said, "What's wrong?"

With renewed fear in her eyes, Cotilda looked up at Slocum. "It's Mary James, the girl I sent to Fort Worth."

Slocum said, "What about her?"

With a shaking finger, Cotilda pointed to a horse that was being led through the camp, toward the town of Parker, by Sheriff Riley. On the mount's back was draped the unmoving slim figure of a girl.

Her voice shaking, Cotilda said, "She was found out in the desert this morning, dead. Shot through the heart. Oh, John, I feel so bad; I thought she would be safe . . ."

Filled with sudden rage, Slocum turned to see Rafer Burns staring with faint interest at the passing spectacle.

"Burns . . . ," Slocum spat.

Burns turned his eyes on Slocum. "Yes, Mr. Slocum?"

"It's going to come down to you and me, Burns," Slocum said, his voice cold as ice. "And when it does, you won't be the winner."

Burns turned his eyes away from both Slocum and the sight of the corpse-bearing horse. He yawned.

"Mr. Slocum," he said, "you might tell my former friend Pokey Johnson that I'll deal with him after the festivities this afternoon. As for you, you'll be dealt with soon enough."

Burns turned back to his practice, ignoring Slocum and Cotilda completely.

And Slocum, still staring at the badman with murderous eyes, said in a cold voice, "That's it, then, Cotilda. There won't be any help from Fort Worth or anywhere else. We're on our own."

19

Ten minutes later, back at the wagering table with Cotilda Murphy, Slocum shook his head.

"I've thought about it five ways from Sunday, Cotilda," Slocum said, "and Burns has us locked in good. If you try to cancel the game this afternoon, Burns, with Sheriff Riley backing him up, will cry fraud, and we'll all be in jail before nightfall. Then Riley can do whatever he wants. We know darn well that if Burns shot Mary James, he either didn't do it with his own pistol or he did it with a firearm that will never be found. There were no witnesses who can help us.

"Riley can't arrest me for the murder since I was already in jail last night. But we both know

they have some sort of plan in place. Their
Mexican accomplices are out there somewhere,
ready to give them backup.

"If we go to Mayor Drucker at this point,
he'll cry foul, too. We both saw him put down
fifty dollars on this baseball game, and like any
betting man, he doesn't want to be cheated out
of losing it. He won't believe us about Sheriff
Riley, because we don't have any direct evidence, and Pokey Johnson is still too scared to
say anything against Rafer Burns.

"Besides, I doubt Burns made any of his most
dangerous plans in front of Pokey to begin
with."

Slocum shook his head. "No, Cotilda, all we
can do is play this baseball game this afternoon, then keep you and your girls safely in
the midst of the good people of Parker, Texas,
while I try to ride out for help."

With tears in her eyes, Cotilda said, "Poor
Mary . . ."

"I know," Slocum said tenderly.

Cotilda looked up suddenly at Slocum.

"And your own plan will never play out,
John. I know Rafer Burns. He'll make sure
you're dead before nightfall, one way or another. And he'll never be caught . . ." Her eyes
stared fearfully.

Slocum said, "I'm not about to let that happen. We'll be surrounded by people the rest of
today—"

Cotilda shook her head. "He'll find a way, John. He always does."

"Then let him try," Slocum said.

As Cotilda was forced to attend to the growing frenetic action of the betting table, Slocum stared with hard eyes toward Rafer Burns, who had gathered his team around him, getting ready for the start of the big game.

"Let him try . . ."

And then—it was time to play ball!

Cotilda's gals, the Fort Worth 'Niners, were now resplendent in their uniforms: a baggy ensemble of shirts and trousers which hid their figures but made them look suddenly much more like ball players.

And Slocum, the lone holdout as far as a uniform was concerned, having insisted that he play the game dressed just as he played the game of life, from boots to hat, was amazed at just how good these 'Niners were when they took the field for practice.

The afternoon was a gorgeous one, with a sharp, hot sun set in a high desert-blue sky. The excited crowd spread down and back from the two base lines, from home plate all the way out to the tall flagged sticks that had been pegged in left and right fields to mark the home runs.

Slocum was put out in Mary James's spot, which was left field, and he managed not to embarrass himself, by catching the couple of balls that were hit out to him.

Most of his attention, though, was paid to Rafer Burns, whose own team looked just as professional during their practice session, drawing huge cheers from the crowd. Burns himself had a private conference with his pitcher, Fontaine, and with two latecomers to the game, two Mexicans dressed in black whom Slocum took an immediate interest in.

After conferring with Burns for a few minutes, the two newcomers took a place in the crowd in left field, leaving them close to Slocum when he played that position.

Studying them carefully, Slocum could see no obvious weaponry on them; at this range, they would have a hard time hitting him with a sidearm, but Slocum would nonetheless have to be aware of the possibility.

After the two short practices had been completed, Mayor Drucker, standing at home plate, called the crowd to attention and spoke.

"Ladies and gentlemen of Parker! This is a great day for our town!" Drucker studied a piece of paper in his hand. "Miss Cotilda Murphy, proprietor of the spectacle you are about to witness, has informed me that the betting has exceeded," he squinted at the piece of paper, bringing it close to his face, "eight hundred gold pieces!"

An appreciative roar went up from the crowd at their own gambling fever.

Drucker held his hand up for silence.

"Now, the rules in this afternoon's competition are simple. The game will be played cleanly, and fairly! To this end, the Reverend Gates, pastor of our church here in Parker, will officiate as umpire. I take it there are no objections to this arrangement?"

Drucker smiled at Rafer Burns's team, lined up along the left base line between home plate and third base, and the Fort Worth 'Niners, similarly arrayed down the other line.

Someone from the crowd shouted out, "Hey, Drucker, how do we know who the Reverend's betting on?"

There was a roar of laughter, and Reverend Gates, face reddening, stepped to Drucker's side and shouted, "I have made no bets at all! As the Good Book says—"

"Aw, that's all right, Reverend!" the man in the crowd called out. "We know you're honest!"

After another roar of laughter, Drucker patted Reverend Gates's arm, assuring him that everything was all right, then quieted the crowd.

"There's nothing more to say then," he said, "except: play ball!"

Now there was a gigantic cheer, in the midst of which Rafer Burns and Cotilda Murphy met with Reverend Gates at home plate, where a gold piece was tossed in the air.

Burns won the toss.

"We'll bat last," he said, smiling in an oily way at Cotilda.

Cotilda, having donned her loose cap, upon which was the emblem of a falcon in flight, nodded brusquely and called her team over, as Burns's boys took the field.

As Burns ran out to his own position at first base, he passed by Slocum and said, quietly enough so that only Slocum could hear, "You'll never make it through this game alive."

20

The first inning went smoothly enough. Cotilda's first two batters reached base and were driven forward to second and third when Cotilda herself hit a bouncing ball that went deep into the hole at second.

The second baseman, a tall and wiry local boy, made a heroic leap as the ball bounced high above him, drawing it down in his glove-less hand and throwing it to Rafer Burns at first.

The Reverend Gates, standing behind the pitcher to gain a view of the entire field, called Cotilda out by the slimmest of margins.

The slight kiss Burns brushed across Cotilda's cheek as she ran by was not lost on the crowd, who hooted, while Reverend Gates blushed.

As Cotilda, burning mad, stalked by, Burns whispered, "By the end of today, there will be nothing but kisses from me for you, my dear."

Cotilda turned her angry eyes on Burns, and the cold certainty in his set features sent a chill down her spine.

"I'd die first," she said.

Burns shrugged slightly. "Either way, Cotilda . . ."

Cotilda stormed away as the next batter came up.

Now the pitcher, Fontaine, went to work. Two pitches were swinging strikes, but then Fontaine took a moment, brushed his fingers back through his hair, and rubbed up the ball before throwing it again. This all looked natural enough, but Cotilda, now standing next to Slocum, said, "Watch what the ball does now."

Slocum watched as the next pitch started in straight enough, then took a crazy, unnatural dip as it reached the batter, who missed it for a third strike.

The next batter met with similar results, and the 'Niners' half of the inning to bat was over.

"Why don't you tell Gates that Fontaine is cheating?" Slocum asked, as he ran out toward his position with Cotilda.

"I've been through this before. Gates would examine the ball and find nothing, and that would be the end of it. Fontaine is an expert at it. But we 'Niners have a few tricks of our own to battle it."

Slocum left Cotilda at the pitcher's mound and ran out to left field, where he observed the Mexicans paying very close attention to him.

Slocum decided to let them know he was aware of them, and turned in their direction, brushing his hand across his Colt and then saluting.

The Mexicans looked at each other, then back at Slocum impassively.

Since Cotilda was still warming up, Slocum decided to make sure he was understood, and trotted over to the Mexicans, drew them aside, and told them, "I just want you to know that if you start anything, I'll finish it."

The two startled men stared at Slocum as he took out his Colt for them to look at.

Slocum stared at them coldly. "My .45's loaded and ready," he said, "and if you make the first move, there are two bullets in here with your names on them."

While he was putting these thoughts in their minds, Slocum was studying them closely. One of them was carrying a pair of .45's of his own, and the other had a knife in his boot, but outside of that they had nothing on them.

"Remember what I said, amigos," Slocum said. "If you stick with Rafer Burns and try anything at all against me or the Fort Worth 'Niners, you'll be in the ground deeper than a cactus before nightfall. It's that simple."

Slocum left the two men pondering his words and went back for the start of the bottom of the first.

The bottom of the first inning went much as the top of the inning had. Cotilda Murphy was every bit as good a pitcher as Fontaine, and didn't have to rely on dirty tricks to get the job done.

The only man to reach base was Fontaine himself, who seemed to know all kinds of ways to cheat, as he knocked the first baseman aside while running out a hit ball, causing her to drop the ball and allowing Reverend Gates to call him safe.

The next batter up was Rafer Burns.

Slocum tensed. He felt that if anything were going to happen this afternoon, it would happen at Burns's signal, and indeed the badman did seem to turn to the two Mexicans in the crowd and nod when he stepped to the plate. Slocum found himself dividing his attention between the game and the Mexicans, but the two men did not move, and soon Burns had been retired on a fly ball to the right fielder.

The second and third innings went much as the first, but in the fourth inning there were some fireworks that set the crowd's juices flowing. With two men on base, Rafer Burns once again stepped to the plate—and once again he seemed to nod toward the two Mexicans. Slocum tried to keep an eye on the two men—but this time Burns hit a towering fly in Slocum's direction and he was forced to take his eye off the two men in the crowd.

Slocum caught the ball, but when he looked back, one of the Mexicans had disappeared.

Slocum swore that Burns had hit the ball toward him deliberately as a diversion.

The next two batters made singles, and though the next batter was retired for the third out of the inning, suddenly the 'Niners were down by the score of two to nothing.

"All right, 'Niners," Cotilda said as her team prepared for the bottom of the inning, "it's time to get something done."

One of the girls said tiredly, "You mean it's time to figure out a way to hit Fontaine's cheat ball!"

Cotilda nodded. "Leave that to me, Lucy."

The first batter of the inning struck out on Fontaine's dipping cheater, but now Cotilda Murphy stepped to the plate.

Holding her bat high, she waited for Fontaine's first pitch.

Sure enough, the dipping cheater came in—but Cotilda dipped her bat with the pitch and swung upward, catching the ball solidly and driving it high and far.

The left fielder ran back in an attempt to follow the ball, but only stopped to watch helplessly as it sailed far beyond his reach, out beyond the pole marks of the outfield for a home run.

Grinning, Cotilda rounded the bases.

"That's how to handle Fontaine's ball," she said, and indeed the next batter followed her example, driving a ball deep over the center field home-run line, to make the score two to two.

The score remained that way for the next four, hard-fought innings. In the bottom of the fifth, Slocum noticed that the second Mexican was back in the crowd, next to his companion, as if he had never left. Slocum kept an eye on the two of them as much as possible, but Rafer Burns made no signal toward them and they seemed content to watch the game.

Slocum made one fine catch in the bottom of the eighth which ended the inning, robbing Fontaine of a home-run ball.

The pitcher eyed him murderously as he walked toward the mound, and Slocum ran in, dropping the ball at Fontaine's feet.

"You up this inning, Slocum?" Fontaine asked.

Slocum nodded. "Yep."

Fontaine gave him a nasty grin. "Watch your head," he said.

Slocum was up first in the 'Niners' top of the ninth, and as Fontaine had promised, the first pitch, a fast ball, came flying at Slocum's head.

The crowd hooted wildly as Slocum dove for the ground, the ball sailing where his cranium had been a second before.

Out behind the pitcher, Reverend Gates frowned unhappily.

Slocum dusted himself off and stood back in the box—and sure enough, the second pitch also came at his head.

Reverend Gates said, "I don't think—"

"Shut up, Padre," Fontaine snapped, and Gates, his face reddening, watched helplessly as the pitcher fired a third ball at Slocum, which Slocum handled by stepping quickly back and swinging his bat at it.

At the crack of the bat, the crowd let out a gasp, and the ball flew high and far, easily clearing the left-center field mark for a home run.

Slocum circled the bases, as Fontaine's eyes followed him like daggers.

"Smile now, Slocum," Fontaine said. "You won't be smiling for long . . ."

The rest of the 'Niners went down in order, falling to Fontaine's dirty pitcher's tricks, and the score stood three to two when Rafer Burns's team came up for their last chance.

The crowd's excitement built as Fontaine, the first batter, reached first base on a close play. The next two batters made out, and then it was Rafer Burns's turn.

In left field, Slocum noticed a heightening of interest on the Mexicans' part. He now found himself torn between the excitement of the game and the certainty that something was about to happen on the part of the Mexicans.

His feelings were only enhanced when Burns stepped out of the batter's box after a second strike and made a motion to the two men, plain for Slocum to see.

On the mound, Cotilda wound up and gave the ball a mighty throw toward the plate. It headed right down the middle.

The crowd drew in its breath as Rafer Burns, concentrating mightily, took a strong swing and sent the ball flying out in Slocum's direction.

At first the ball, high as it was, looked like an easy home run, but its height slowed down its length of travel, and Slocum, well in front of the home-run line, settled under it to make an easy catch and end the game in the 'Niners favor.

At that moment a rifle shot split the air, and Slocum felt the uncomfortable hot sting of a bullet.

Suddenly his vision began to blur, and the ball falling toward him disappeared into the blue afternoon sky, and the world began to go away.

And then Slocum was falling, and the ball was falling in front of him as he heard the crowd, not realizing what had happened to Slocum, react to the fact that Rafer Burns and Fontaine were scoring, and that the town of Parker's team had won the game.

And John Slocum was on the ground—shot!

21

Even as Slocum hit the ground, he knew that the Mexican with the rifle was aiming a second shot at him. The man must have retrieved a rifle when he had left at Burns's signal back in the fourth inning.

Slocum, still groggy, nevertheless reacted with the catlike reflexes that had saved his life a hundred times before.

Rolling to the side, he heard the second shot go off, spitting dirt behind him.

Slocum pushed himself to his hands and knees and shook his head, clearing it. His right eye saw a clarifying blur, and as Slocum ran his hand quickly across it, he realized that the bullet had only grazed his face near the eye.

There was no time to think about how lucky he'd been. Slocum's left eye worked perfectly, and now he saw the two Mexicans in the startled crowd, one of them aiming his rifle for a third shot.

Almost without thinking, Slocum drew his Colt across his body and fired in one smooth motion.

The Mexican holding the rifle went down even as he fired his third shot, which bit the sand harmlessly in front of Slocum.

The other Mexican immediately drew his revolver, but he was dead before he aimed it at Slocum, who drilled him through the chest.

Slocum turned to see Rafer Burns at home plate, holding Cotilda Murphy with a Colt pointed at her head!

Beside Burns was Fontaine, just drawing his own .45 from his holster.

"Slocum!" Fontaine snarled, but Slocum had already sent a bullet his way, which found Fontaine's heart before he had pulled off a single shot.

Burns, wild-eyed, shouted, "I'll shoot her right here, Slocum!"

Slocum, gun ready, advanced on the badman, step by step.

"Stop right now, Slocum! I'm not joking!"

Seeing the terror in Cotilda's eyes, and knowing that Burns was mad enough to do what he said, Slocum stopped.

Burns gave him a wide grin.

"I knew you'd do what I said, Slocum! Everybody sooner or later does what I say!"

To Slocum's right, Sheriff Riley emerged from the crowd and said, "There's nowhere to go with this, Burns. It's over for all of us."

"Are you crazy, Riley?" Burns laughed. "I can do whatever I want! Do you think it makes any difference to me that all these townspeople are witnesses? I'll kill them all! I'll burn the town down! No one has ever caught me at anything, and no one ever will!"

Riley shook his head. "Forget it, Burns. It's hopeless."

Burns laughed. "Not at all! I'll bring these girls to Mexico myself. You can still help me if you want to, Riley—we'll go fifty-fifty. All we have to do is take care of Parker, Texas, and Slocum here . . ."

"No way, Burns."

Burns, smiling, stared at Sheriff Riley and then shrugged.

"Have it your way, then, Riley."

Before the sheriff could react, Burns had quickly turned the Colt from Cotilda's head and shot the lawman dead.

"Ha!" Burns said, swiveling the gun back at Cotilda. "Anybody else want to try?"

"How about you and me, Burns?" Slocum said, still aiming his .45 at the badman but unable to get a shot.

Burns shook his head. "I'm not that stupid, Slocum. What I'm going to do now is take Cotilda here and ride off. She's all I ever wanted out of this deal, anyway. I have the money the Mexicans gave me for all the girls. I can live off that for a long time." His wild grin widened. "And I have Cotilda."

"I'd rather die, Burns," Cotilda said.

Burns said, "I hope not, my dear. But if that's the only way . . ."

Moving slowly, he began to drag Cotilda toward a nearby mount. To Slocum he said, "Go ahead, hero—take a shot! She'll be dead before I am!"

Burns began to laugh, nearly at the horse. There was nothing Slocum could do, because he knew that Burns would surely kill Cotilda if he tried anything.

Burns threw back his head and howled. "And remember—I'll be back for all of you! The town of Parker will never be safe! And I'll get you, too, Slocum!"

In mid-laugh, as he maneuvered Cotilda to his side to push her up on the horse, gun still held tightly against her, Burns suddenly stopped laughing.

A gunshot had gone off behind him, and now Burns, amazed, looked down at his middle to see a spurt of blood rise out through his chest.

"Who . . . ," he said, turning in wonder as a second shot hit him, this time in the front.

Burns collapsed to the ground, dropping his own weapon, a look of surprise forever frozen on his face.

He tried to say his mortal wounder's name, but was unable to pronounce the word before his lips were stilled by death.

"That's right," Pokey Johnson said coldly, all traces of his nervous stutter gone as he stood over the cold body of the vicious killer Rafer Burns. "It was me, Pokey. And I shot you in the back, just like you shot all those others in the back. It was me, and now you won't ever kill or bother anyone ever again."

In the crowd, pandemonium broke out. The excitement of Parker winning the baseball contest, followed by the commotion of the last few minutes, was all too much for the normally sleepy town.

For his heroics, Pokey Johnson was lifted on the shoulders of those nearby and paraded around to cheers while La Vonda looked admiringly on.

Slocum found Cotilda Murphy in his arms.

"Oh, John, it's over!" she cried.

"Yes," Slocum said, "it is."

"And thank God you're safe!"

Slocum said, "I was worried about you for a few moments there, until Pokey came along."

Cotilda gazed longingly up into Slocum's eyes.

"The baseball game's over now, John. And I

did miss being with you last night . . ."

Mayor Drucker, wearing a stunned and happy smile on his face, came by and stopped before Cotilda.

"I've been speaking with Reverend Gates about how best to resolve our various situations," he said, "and I believe we've come up with a solution, Miss Murphy. There's the matter of the game winnings, of course, and also the matter of the money which was found on Rafer Burns's body. If—"

"That'll have to wait, Mayor," Cotilda said, not taking her hungry eyes from Slocum's. "John Slocum and I have an abandoned mine to explore."

22

Leaving the befuddled mayor far behind, Slocum and Cotilda had their clothes off nearly before they reached the entrance of the abandoned mine.

Cotilda became a wild, possessed thing, planting kisses all over Slocum before easing him onto his back, spreading his legs, and on her hands and knees, taking his already hardening cock into her mouth.

Slocum's dick quickly hardened completely as her expert tongue and lips worked his shaft. Already a pressure was mounting in Slocum's balls, tightening toward eventual explosion, and he closed his eyes as her wet mouth oiled his cock to perfection.

Sliding her tongue up to his cockhead, she slipped his member from her lips and leaned up to whisper needfully in Slocum's ear.

"John, I can feel you're ready . . . Do you want to give it now?"

Her wish was evident, and Slocum said, "There's plenty to go around, ma'am."

Moaning at the ecstasy to come, Cotilda pulled her licking tongue back down Slocum's chest and belly before sliding it back down over his red-hard dick.

As she worked it perfectly, Slocum was ready to give her what she wanted in no time. As she opened her mouth to lick up to the tip of the shaft, she moaned the word "Now . . ." and then lowered her lips tightly around Slocum's cock, taking it deep into her mouth.

Slocum felt his balls tighten and then release, sending a hot, streaming torrent of cum up into her waiting mouth.

Moaning in the back of her throat, Cotilda swallowed as fast as she could handle it as shot after shot of whiteness jerked over her tongue. Her own middle was wettening in her excitement, and she felt the first tremble of a roaring orgasm, which hit her even as Slocum's continued. Her own juice ran down her leg as a final shot of lovely white seed shot into her throat.

She brought her lips up to the top of Slocum's

cock shaft and licked the remains of whiteness that clung slickly there.

Now, lying back herself, still licking at her lips and feeling the remains of her own first orgasm, she panted for Slocum to rise over her and give her more, this time below.

"You . . . said . . . there was plenty . . . to go around . . . ," she panted.

Slocum's spent cock was already recharging, hardening at the sight of this moaning, ready woman, legs spread, moist middle heaving toward him in need.

In a moment, Slocum's cock was red and ready once more, and he slid it long and hard and deep into Cotilda.

"Oh!" Cotilda cried, feeling Slocum's length fill her completely.

And then they became as one organism, a writhing, moaning thing with a core of wet heat that built and built, and Slocum rode and rode her as afternoon became evening . . .

"Give it to me now, John!" she cried, after what seemed an eternity of wild riding.

And Slocum obliged her, his balls once again unwinding a tremendous torrent of cum-seed, driving the hot flood up deep into Cotilda as she felt once again her own orgasm flying free from within her, racking her body with wet, white, hot juice which slammed against Slocum's seed within her, driving her nearly to madness as her cries echoed down the empty passages of the mine tunnel—

"Yes! Oh God yes! Yes, John!"

And still the twin orgasms continued, cum driving hotly against cum, Slocum's rock-hard dick pumping mightily until Cotilda was driven nearly mad with the pleasure of it—

"Yesssss!"

And, with a mighty last blast that ended at just the right time, suddenly it was over, and Cotilda had collapsed in Slocum's arms.

"Oh, John," she whispered happily, "that was like nothing I've ever felt. That was . . . wonderful . . ."

And then, looking sleepily out at the darkening sky, she was asleep, and Slocum, having to agree, found his own eyes growing heavy, and soon was asleep beside her.

And then, all too soon, morning had come, and Slocum awoke to find himself alone, his clothes covering him like a blanket.

He stood, stretched, dressed, and walked out to the sight of the Fort Worth 'Niners packed and ready to leave.

The baseball field had been dismantled, the bases and outfield stakes pulled up, the sand and dirt brushed into the waiting desert, leaving no sign that a ball field had ever been there.

The wagons were packed, except for the griddle, which lay waiting for Slocum with La Vonda in attendance.

"Slocum!" she called happily, smiling. "I've been waiting on you! Get on over here and have one more stack of my flapjacks before I pack up!"

Slocum ambled over and in no time was sitting with a steaming cup of coffee and a tall stack of cakes.

"Good as ever, La Vonda," he said.

"You bet they are!" she said.

Slocum indicated the wagons. "Where you off to next?"

La Vonda's smile widened. "Me? I'm staying right here in Parker. Pokey's been asked to stay on here as sheriff—and he's asked me to be his wife!"

Slocum grinned. "I'm happy to hear that, La Vonda."

"Things worked out, just like you said. The Reverend Gates is going to do the ceremony next Sabbath. Pokey's a good man, and I'll make him a good wife."

"I'm sure you will, La Vonda. What about the rest of the 'Niners?"

La Vonda pointed to Cotilda Murphy, who was approaching them, smiling.

"I'll let her tell you," La Vonda said. She leaned over and gave Slocum a kiss on the cheek. "Thanks, Slocum," she said, and then she made herself busy with the wagon, leaving Slocum and Cotilda alone.

"Good morning, John," Cotilda said, smiling.

"Good morning yourself. Getting ready to move on?"

She nodded. "I settled up with Mayor Drucker. The town of Parker officially won the baseball game, so they split the winnings. Needless to say, they're happy."

"And you get nothing?"

"Quite the contrary," Cotilda said. "The mayor decided that we should have the money that was found on Rafer Burns. There was a thousand dollar bill for every one of my girls. The mayor called it blood money, and said the only way to wash it was to give it to us."

"What are you going to do with it?"

"I talked it over with the girls. We've given a thousand to La Vonda and Pokey, and we'll send a thousand of it back to Mary James's family. With the rest of it we've decided to go back east, replace the players we've lost, and start a league."

"A woman's baseball league?"

"Why not? If there can be such a thing as a National League for men, why not for women? If it doesn't happen now, it will someday."

She moved closer to Slocum and took his arm in her firm yet loving grip.

"A thousand dollars is also yours, John," she said. "You could throw in your lot with us. Be president of the league, if you want."

Slocum smiled. "You know I'd be no good for that."

"Not enough action?"

"Something like that."

Cotilda sighed, then smiled.

"I'll miss you, John Slocum," she said.

"I'll miss you, too, Cotilda."

She pressed her hand against Slocum's palm, and left a thousand dollar bill there.

"Thanks," she said. She leaned closer, brushing Slocum's cheek with her lips. "For everything," she whispered.

She kissed him lightly, then turned away and readied the wagons to leave.

Slocum watched them move off a little while later. They left much as they had come, with a dusty trail kicked up by their wheels, two wagons filled with girls, and a game that would become a national pastime. On his Appaloosa, ready to ride out himself, with a thousand dollars in his poke now and another little town waiting for him somewhere, Slocum waved as the wagons pulled away.

Suddenly they stopped, and Cotilda Murphy jumped down from the lead wagon and turned to face Slocum.

As the dust settled around her, she suddenly reared her hand back and threw mightily.

Something white and round sailed through the air, and Slocum reached out his hand and caught a new baseball.

"Something to remember me by!" Cotilda called, and then she climbed back up into the wagon, snapped the reins, and soon was gone in a cloud of desert dust.

Sitting there in his saddle, Slocum studied the ball, realizing just how much it had done for him.

Three days ago, he had been bored silly, sleeping in the desert, in the shadow of his own horse, unaware of danger and ready for nothing.

Today he had a full poke and felt alive again, ready for anything.

"Thanks," Slocum said, tossing the ball up once in the air and catching it.

He packed it carefully away in his saddlebag, then gently spurred his Appaloosa, to ride out on the road that would take him somewhere else.

Wherever it was, he was ready for it.

Turn the page for a special
preview of the next
SLOCUM adventure . . .

BOOMTOWN SHOWDOWN

Slocum rides into a powderkeg of a town . . .
where greed and gold dust
will light the fuse!

No moon. Save for the small cluster of twinkling lights, Not-a-Chance, Wyoming, lay shrouded in the dark of night. Yet from the top of the long deep draw, John Slocum, astride the chunky, often feisty Appaloosa, let his careful gaze slip over the group of mute frame-houses, log cabins, and half-dozen tents. He could feel in his muscled, yet supple body the thinning night as it stretched toward the pre-dawn; while maintaining for those strange moments its essential darkness. At the same time he was taking in the fact that the cluster of light at the south end of town had to be coming from the cribs in the cabbage patch. He could almost feel the sound of revelry in his listening body, realizing its strong pull. Yet only for a moment. Only when the light wind stirred, bringing the smell of recently departed rain. Now leaning on the pommel of his stock saddle, he listened to the surrounding silence of the thin mountain night.

He sat absolutely still, moving only with the slight change in the Appaloosa as that tough little horse bent his head to crop at the short buffalo grass. The horse's bit jangled with each crunch of those strong, cupped teeth.

Now, wishing for a finer silence, Slocum lifted the horse's head with a slight pull on the reins, and both man and animal felt further into the night.

Something? His listening widened with the increasing softening of his body. He was certain that he'd lost the pair who'd been backtrailing him; yet he had not lost his caution. For sure John Slocum knew a man didn't get old in the big country by being dumb.

He loosened himself more, letting his attention fill every part of him, from the top of his head all the way down through his fingers to his feet.

Shifting his weight carefully so that there would be no creaking of leather and no surprise for the horse, John Slocum held the reins to avoid any tossing of the animal's head that would cause the metal bit to jangle, and he kneed the tough Appaloosa into a careful walk.

He knew he'd lost his trackers, but he also knew there could be others. Intentional, or by accident, there was always the chance of someone cutting his trail. Especially now.

Moving his left arm he felt the slight stiffness in his shoulder where the bullet had creased him, not doing any serious damage. A Spencer repeater, he was pretty sure.

He'd been following a fresh deer trail just at nightfall, as it lined a narrow, winding creek; a good piece east and south of Not-a-Chance. The sun had just gone down, but there was still the shadowy light of the dying day. He'd felt the warning, something like a tug inside himself; a message that he knew well for it had saved him more than once or twice in the past. And even as the wicked crack of the Spencer had confirmed his premonition he had already kicked the Appaloosa into a gallop, lying low over the horse's flying mane. Just making it to the stand of cottonwoods that was bunched in a sharp curve further up the creek. It was only then that he realized he'd been hit.

In the cover of the trees he had waited, searching his back trail. But the light was no good for him, and he could hear only the slight stirring of air in the branches of the cottonwoods.

He had waited for a follow-up, but none came. A warning shot, was it? He'd discounted any sort of accident. He knew it had been directed at him. Had he gotten too close to somebody's range? Or maybe it was just some nervous sonofabitch with fear in his fingers. Not too likely. He was pretty damned sure that bullet had been meant for John Slocum.

He had known early on that somebody was on his back trail; picking up on it just after he'd ridden not too far out of Stone Teats down below the big Pitchfork spread. An outrider from one of the big outfits? Or was it someone who knew why he was riding to Not-a-Chance in the Little Horn country?

Actually, he'd thought of the possibility of trouble even before he'd left Stone Teats following his meeting with Mace Terringer. It was only to be expected that somebody would be interested in his moves. For sure, it was known by more than just one or two that he'd been meeting with Terringer at the Frontier House. And it could have been someone sent by Terringer himself just to "keep him honest." It was a favorite tactic of Terringer's—a man he could trust no farther than he could reach; or as old Lars Nelson had put it, " 'bout as far as a man can piss into a hurricane in the middle of winter."

Old Lars—likely eighty now going on ninety, and for sure still sharp as a blade, tough as the handle on a pitchfork.

Old Lars had been a real education; teaching him stuff that a whole lot more often than not had stood him in damn good stead. He wondered if that old man was still about. He by God could be. But no matter where he turned up, Slocum knew he'd be telling them how to "take and do it," telling them to "quit staring the spots off them cards, and play 'em, by God!" As far as John Slocum was concerned, old Lars Nelson was the only kind of school there was—the kind walking around on legs and feet. He would sure like to see that old-timer again.

Well, no matter. That drygulcher had nicked him. Slocum, being Slocum, had to fight himself not to go after the sonofabitch right now. Hell, a warning shot didn't have to crease his shoulder. 'Course, the man might've been trying to hit him. And why hadn't he followed up? Afraid of getting too close? Was he somebody Slocum would've known?

He dropped it. He was not a man to pick at thoughts. He had a rule of simply thinking something through and then leaving it; not forgetting it, but not allowing it to eat him, to deplete his attention with endless ruminating the way a good many men were in the habit of doing. By golly, more than a few of such were now planted on account of when they should have been topping out the action they'd been "turning it over."

Now he waited while the Appaloosa bobbed his head, biting down at a tick near his right shoulder, his bit jangling.

Slocum pressed his right boot heel into the horse's ribs, and they started along the thin trail leading down to the little town, quartering down the long draw, making sure not to throw any outline against the night sky. And as he rode now he kept his right hand within inches of his holstered six-gun. He had already loosened the Winchester in its saddle boot.

Now in the dark his eyes sharpened as they became one with the changing light. He knew how to see even when there wasn't any light, having learned it from an old Cherokee, and then also from old Lars Nelson. He also had a natural talent for seeing what was actually there in front of him, and behind too, without giving way to imagination.

Slocum, who a number of people thought had Indian in him—and indeed looked it with his jet-black hair and piercing black eyes— knew how to see in the dark, how to listen through the silence; for he was a man who had always known the wisdom of trusting his senses, his instincts, and did not rely on his head alone. His articulate and total body-sense allowed him to participate in the world that lay beyond observation; a world few white men knew.

Riding down to the little town, he was well aware of the fact that he was indeed exposed, even in the night. Not-a-Chance, either by purpose or not, was situated so that no one could approach its environs without being seen—by day *or* by night.

He had no trouble finding the livery. He bedded the Appaloosa with a good rubdown and ample feed, and threw his duffle on a pile of fresh hay in the loft that gave a clear view of both barn doors. And with one eye open, he slept, as dawn began to touch that leathery little town.

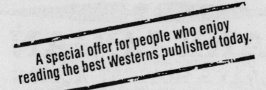